1

Impossible
Wizard

JAMES E. WISHER

James E. Wisher

The Aegis of Merlin:

The Impossible Wizard

The Awakening

The Chimera Jar

The Raven's Shadow

Edited by: Janie Linn Dullard

Cover Art by: Paganus

Sand Hill Publishing 410171.0

ISBN 13: 978-1-945763-07-6

Chapter 1

Tests

"Love you, Mom Gotta go "

The apartment door slammed behind Conryu, cutting off his mother in mid harangue It wasn't like he didn't know he'd gotten up late The hall outside was empty, all the residents having gone to work hours ago Mom had only stayed home because she had some research to do for the Science Department and could do it as well at their apartment, saving herself the commute It was just Conryu's luck that the one morning this week he overslept she decided to work from home

He sighed and sprinted down the drab beige hall toward the stairwell The elevator took too long for just four floors He found the stairwell as empty as the hall so he had no trouble rushing up to the penthouse three steps at a time If anybody had seen him right then they'd have thought the building had caught fire

Conryu skidded to a halt on the top landing and paused to catch his breath Four flights of steps wasn't so many, but at three to a stride his legs were swearing at him a little. He straightened his t-shirt and gave a little sniff to make sure he hadn't overwhelmed his deodorant. All good.

Bad enough he arrived late, if he showed up at Maria's door stinking too she'd really let him have it. Satisfied that he was as put together as he could manage, Conryu yanked the steel fire door open and stepped into the hall that led to the Kane family's penthouse apartment

Burnished oak paneling covered the walls and soft tan carpet silenced the tread of his leather biker boots. A jade vase filled with fresh-cut roses sat on a small table and filled the air with their fragrant perfume. At the end of the hall a tall set of double doors carved with symbols and a pair of pentagrams marked the entrance to the Kanes' apartment.

Maria's mom oversaw the wards protecting the building from magical and mundane threats and the doors served as a sort of anchor. She'd tried to explain the process to him once, but it went right over his head. All Conryu knew for sure was that in exchange for her magical protections the Kanes got the best apartment in the building rent free. Pretty sweet deal.

He strode past the elevator and paused before the doors. Every time he touched one of the creepy things he feared it would burn his hand off. It hadn't happened yet and he doubted today would be the day. He rapped twice and clasped his hands behind his back.

Half a minute later the door opened and he looked down into the jade eyes of Maria's mother, Shizuku. The short, slender woman's eyes crinkled when she smiled at Conryu. She wore a red silk kimono embroidered with storks that looked like it cost more than all the clothes Conryu owned Midnight-blue slippers peeked out from the bottom of the robe Shizuku Kane was one of the most talented wizards in the city, but he'd always thought of her like a second mother

"You're late, Conryu "

"Yeah How mad is she?"

"This is your lucky day Maria's still getting ready "

Conryu's eyebrows shot up Maria was never late Ever "Really?"

"Don't look so shocked This is a big day for her For all the girls It's no surprise she wants to look her best for Testing Day "

Conryu sighed Testing Day A big deal for the girls and a waste of time for the boys They would all take the test of course; couldn't have anyone feeling left out What did it matter if boys couldn't become wizards? Fair's fair after all

The truth was, most of the girls wouldn't pass either When they tested the seniors last year, only two out of the whole class of three hundred and sixty-seven had passed and gotten a full ride at the North American Alliance's Arcane Academy All Conryu and the other boys would get was hours of standing in line and a sneer of disdain from the woman administering the test

The patter of shoes on hardwood reached him a moment before the whirlwind that was Maria Kane appeared behind her mother She rushed to the door in a swirl of black skirts, her purse over one shoulder, and paused to kiss her mother on the cheek She grabbed his hand and dragged him towards the elevator

"Nice seeing you, Mrs Kane," Conryu called over his shoulder

Maria jabbed her finger into the call button. When the door didn't open at once she stabbed it again and again.

Finally Conryu grabbed her free hand and held it. "Relax. We'll make it in plenty of time."

Maria looked up at him with her liquid brown eyes. She was only three inches taller than her mother and had the same long black hair. "Relax? How can I relax? Today will make or break my whole life. If I don't pass the test and get into the academy…"

"I know, I know. You've talked about nothing else for the past month"

The elevator bell chimed and the doors slid open. Conryu let go of her hand, stepped inside, and punched the button for the parking garage.

When the doors slid shut he continued, "Even if you don't pass—"

She made a choking sound and stared at him, aghast.

Conryu grimaced. Maybe he wasn't helping. "What I'm trying to say is with your grades you can get a full ride at any college you want to attend. You can do anything you put your mind to. I know you'll be disappointed, but it really won't be the end of the world."

She groaned and hugged him. A muffled "thanks" barely reached his ears. She stepped back and stared at him. "I'm going to pass"

He smiled and nodded. If sheer willpower affected the test, she'd have no problems. "Of course."

The elevator chimed and the doors slid open revealing the almost-empty garage. Conryu led the way to his bike. When he saw her he smiled. She had a sleek black tank and fenders, fully rebuilt flat-head motor, and the coolest skull-and-chain license plate holder

Maria walked past him, pulling him along as she went "Stop drooling I swear every time you see that bike you act like it's the first time "

Conryu let her drag him across the garage Their helmets dangled from the handlebars and he handed Maria hers before buckling his on He settled into his seat and she swung up behind him The soft leather creaked under him as Conryu got comfortable He touched the starter button and the flat-head roared to life, sending a vibration through his whole body

God, he loved that sound

Maria swatted him on the side of his helmet, her less-than-subtle signal that it was time to go He twisted the throttle and roared up the ramp and into the bright sunlight The shining steel-and-glass skyline of Sentinel City spread out before them Beyond the city, little more than a shimmer, was the Atlantic Ocean

Conryu shot down a side street then merged with the endless traffic running along the main thoroughfare that would take them to school It was only ten miles, but their late start would make it a near thing Maria's grip tightened around his middle when he opened the throttle He loved the highway; no speed limit

About halfway to school they rode through a shadow spreading across the street Conryu glanced up The floating island made its patient way through the sky, as indifferent to them as the earth itself Which reminded him

"We're still on for the Shadow Carnival this weekend, right?" He had to shout to be sure she heard him over the roar of the bike.

"Of course, it's our last one as juveniles. Next year we'll have to pay full price "

Conryu snorted For someone from such a rich family, Maria worried a lot about money. Full price at the carnival only cost ten bucks.

They reached the ugly, tan stone school in five minutes, giving them a whole three to spare. Conryu pulled into the first open parking space he came to, put the kickstand down, and swung his leg off. Plenty of cars in the lot, but no people. The seniors must have started lining up already

Maria hopped down, handed him her helmet, and started fussing with her hair. Conryu shook his head and hung their helmets from the handlebars. Maria was the most beautiful girl in school and the windblown hair only added to her looks.

"Maria!" A slightly pudgy blond girl in too-tight jeans, her cleavage threatening to spill out of a low-cut blouse, ran toward them waving her hand.

Maria looked up and smiled. "Rin."

"Come on, the government wizard is here already and the girls are lining up. If we don't hurry we'll be last."

Conryu watched Maria and Rin run ahead to find places in line. So enthusiastic, you'd think your place in line had some bearing on the results. He gave his bike one last affectionate pat and ambled toward the main entrance.

They didn't have classes today. Everyone had taken their finals already. Only the seniors actually needed to show up to take the wizard's test. They'd also get their final report cards and find out if they'd qualified for their chosen college.

He ran up a short flight of steps, waved to some underclassmen he recognized from shop, and pushed the heavy glass doors open. Why anyone would come to school if they didn't have to was beyond him. At least two of the juniors were dating seniors. They'd probably tagged along to provide moral support

The day should only last a few hours, but since a government wizard was in charge they'd probably be here until mid-afternoon. Dad liked to say the one thing you could count on was the slowness of the government. His father actually meant it as a compliment since it usually took the council years to screw something up

He had barely stepped through the doors when a familiar voice said, "You're late, bro."

Conryu turned to find Jonny Salazar, his best friend after Maria, strolling toward him, hands thrust into the pockets of his torn jeans.

"Not my fault. Maria was late getting ready."

Jonny raised a fist and Conryu bumped it. "I call bullshit on that one "

Conryu made a little X over his heart. "Swear to god. She was still primping for the test. Like the shoes she wore would make any difference to the wizard."

"Girls. I tell you man, they're all loco."

Conryu grinned

"But we love them anyway," the boys said in unison.

When the laughter subsided Conryu asked, "Where did she set up?"

"Nurse's office." Jonny started doWn the deserted hall. "We're going to be last in line."

"So What? They alWays take the boys last anyWay and each test takes, What, tWo minutes? At least they're not going to give us any homeWork."

"Amen, bro."

The test line snaked doWn the hall and around the bend, ending in front of the library. TWo girls sat at one of the tables pretending to read, but really checking out a couple of guys in varsity athletics jackets four ahead of Jonny.

They took a step forWard as the line advanced. "You still going to Waste your time going to that rinky-dink vocational school?"

"You bet. TWo years and I get my mechanic's license. Mr. McShane has a place for me the day after I graduate and his shop is only tWo blocks from Dad's dojo. TWo of the things I love most in the World, bikes and kung fu, Within Walking distance of each other. HoW could that not be perfect?"

Jonny shook his head. They'd had this argument at least ten times in the last three months, but it seemed his friend Wanted to have one more go around. "I'm telling you, man, you should go to the military academy With me. You love to fight and you've got the brains for it if you just put in more than a half-assed effort."

Conryu yaWned, stretched, and took another step. "Fighting in a tournament is different than fighting in the army."

"Different hoW?" Jonny demanded, hands on hips.

"For one thing, no one at the tournaments actually wants to kill me. Not to mention there are no guns."

"Details, man. Just imagine, after graduation we're posted to patrol a beach in Florida, protecting bikini girls from the zombies that occasionally wash up on shore. You just know how grateful they'd be." Jonny hugged himself and made kissing noises, fully immersed in his delusion.

Conryu smiled at his friend's overactive imagination. Only the sons of generals and others with connections got soft postings like that. "Picture this, Jonny. We graduate and get sent to the northern border where it drops to sixty below at night and the girls don't wear bikinis. We'd spend every day dressed in seven layers of clothes, hunting white drakes and ice wolves if we were lucky and frost giants if we weren't."

"Why do you have to shit on my dreams, dude?"

"Or how about this?" Conryu went on without mercy. "We get posted instead to the southern garrison where it's 120 in the shade and we fight insane, half-human demon worshipers who'd like nothing so much as to cut your heart out as an offering to some monster whose name you can't even pronounce. Sorry, bro. It's bikes and kung fu for me."

"Wuss." Jonny offered him a good-natured grin then turned to watch as a quartet of girls walked by, their heads hanging. Looked like they failed the test.

"Wuss, huh? How about we head over to the dojo when we're finished and spar for a few rounds?"

Jonny waved his hands. "No, man, I'll pass."

"Come on. I heard you made brown belt last month at your dojo."

"Yeah, and I heard you got a fifth band on your black belt and your dad made you assistant instructor. If I want to get my ass kicked I'd prefer it was by a stranger."

Conryu raised an eyebrow. "Wuss."

Jonny shook his head. "Cold, dude, stone cold."

An hour later they'd made it around the bend and the entrance to the nurse's office came into view. Conryu could just make out the back of Maria's head. She wasn't the last girl in line, but she was close. If she failed he just knew she'd blame him.

* * *

A bead of sweat ran down the back of Maria's neck before her already damp blouse absorbed it. Six people to go and it would be her turn Her hands trembled and she had to pee so bad she feared she'd burst. She just had to pass.

Another girl came out of the nurse's office, head hanging, slumped and trudging. The wizard administering the test hadn't passed a single girl and only ten of them remained standing in line. Last year had been a bad year, with only two passing. At the rate they were going, this year would end up worse yet. She took a deep breath and let it out slowly, trying to picture her stress rushing out with the air like Conryu had taught her.

Maria smiled when she thought about Conryu. He was the closest thing she had to a brother or boyfriend, depending how she felt on a particular day. Her mom and his dad had grown up in the same village in the Empire of the Rising Sun She and Conryu had been born within a week of each other and actually came home from the hospital on the same day. It seemed like since that day they hadn't been apart for more than a week at a time. How would she manage a whole school year away from him?

Another somber girl emerged and Maria took a step forward. Five to go. Rin's hands touched the back of her blouse prompting her to turn around. Her best friend looked down at her with wide blue eyes.

"Do you think they'll fail everyone?" Rin spoke Maria's thoughts out loud

"No, I'm going to pass." Maria spoke with a great deal more conviction than she felt

A high-pitched squeal was followed by a brown-haired girl in a short plaid skirt and white blouse dancing out of the office. It was Kimmy Morrow. Maria didn't know the girl well, but she had the third-highest GPA in their class. If anyone else had a chance of getting picked it didn't surprise Maria that Kimmy would be chosen.

"That's one," Rin muttered.

"Kimmy, what'd you pull?" Maria asked. Most people considered it rude to ask a wizard's power level, but Maria couldn't resist.

Kimmy stopped dancing and grinned. "Nine fifty."

Maria nodded. A respectable result, almost exactly at the fiftieth percentile. "Congratulations."

"Thanks, and good luck." Kimmy continued her spinning dance down the hall, drawing the boys' gazes to the occasional glimpse of her underwear.

Maria couldn't blame her for getting excited. Kimmy had just joined an elite group. When Maria passed she'd be equally excited, but she certainly would not be dancing down the hall flashing her panties for the whole school to see.

The rest of the girls ahead of her went quickly in and out with no more passing. Then Maria's turn arrived. She took one last steadying breath then stepped into the nurse's office. A folding table had been set up in the front room beside a White cabinet marked With a red cross. A draWn curtain hid the four cots in the back section of the office. A pale Woman in gray robes, her face lined With deep Wrinkles, sat on the far side of the table.

In front of the government Wizard rested the simple device that Would determine Maria's future. It consisted of nothing more than a Wooden rectangle With a gauge in the center that ran from 0 to 10,000. An extension With a vertical grip jutted out from the base toWard the empty chair.

Maria tried to sWalloW, but found her throat too dry. She clenched her fists to stop the shaking of her hands.

The Wizard looked up at her With a bland expression. "Sometime today Would be good."

"Sorry." Maria dried her hands on her skirt, sat across from the Wizard, and nodded.

"Grasp the handle," the Wizard said.

"Right or left hand?"

The older Woman groaned. "One of the Women in your family is a Wizard, isn't she?"

"Yes, ma'am. My mother. HoW did you knoW?"

"All the girls from families With Wizards are the same. They all Want to make sure they do everything perfectly, afraid if they make a single mistake they Won't pass."

Maria Winced at the flaWless description of her emotions. Had the Wizard used a spell on her?

"Let me tell you something, kid." She gestured at the device on the table betWeen them. "All this thing does is give a rough measure of how much magical energy your body can process. That's it. Anything over a hundred means you can cast at least simple spells and you need to go to the academy to be trained. Now grab the damn thing and let's get this show on the road "

Maria found the woman's indifferent attitude exactly what she needed to alleviate her nerves. The wizard had done this thousands of times and found the process ordinary to the point of tedium. This might be the most important day of Maria's life, but to the wizard it was just another day at work. Somehow that took all the pressure off.

She grasped the handle with her right hand and stared at the gauge

Nothing happened

The seconds ticked by like hours as the little red needle sat frozen at zero.

Maria's heart raced.

This couldn't be happening. She squeezed until her knuckles turned white.

Move!

Damn it, move!

"Sorry, miss," the wizard began.

The needle twitched.

"Did you see it?" Maria asked, the relief palpable in her voice

"Yeah. Let's give it a couple more seconds."

The needle twitched again then climbed. 100. 200. Steadily on past 1,000.

When it passed 1,500 Maria's head spun and it took all her focus not to let out a hysterical laugh That put her in the ninetieth percentile

It continued on before finally stopping at 1,950. She'd finished fifty points higher than her mother.

"Congratulations, kid. You're going to the academy."

Maria peeled her aching hand off the grip. A red, curved impression ran the length of her palm. She rubbed the mark and smiled. "What happens now?"

"You get out of here so I can test the next girl. The Department of Magic Will send you something in the mail before the end of the summer that'll explain the rest of the process. Now scoot."

Maria hopped out of the chair. She had to tell Conryu.

* * *

"I pulled nineteen fifty." Maria quivered With excitement. Conryu couldn't remember ever seeing her this Worked up.

"Congratulations."

Jonny gave her a thumbs up. "AWesome."

"Thanks. I need to call Mom." She spun to go then turned back. "You guys Want to go to Giovanni's for pizza after to celebrate? My treat."

The test must have damaged her brain. Maria never offered to pick up the check. "I'm in."

"Me too." Jonny never passed up a free meal, let alone free pizza.

"Great. I'll meet you by the bike." Maria Walked off, digging through her purse.

When she'd gone Jonny asked, "Is nineteen fifty good?"

"If she volunteered to buy lunch it must be fantastic. Savor this pizza, Jonny. She may never offer again." They shared a laugh.

The last four girls took their turns, but none of them passed. The boys came next. Each one was in and out in about thirty seconds. An hour later Jonny came out and shrugged. "Hurry up. I'm starving."

Conryu entered the office. Instead of Nurse Abrams with her long legs and ridiculous heels he found a withered old woman in gray robes sitting behind a cheap folding table holding some contraption. Would it have killed them to send a nice-looking wizard to administer the test?

"You the last one?" she asked.

"Yeah "

"Sit down and grab the handle."

Conryu plopped into the plastic chair and grabbed the dowel. The little needle on the gauge snapped over to 10,000.

"Oh, come on." The wizard rapped the device twice with a gold ring just above the swollen knuckle of her right middle finger. The needle didn't move. "Cheap piece of junk. Let go."

Conryu did as she said, not at all certain what was going on. "Can I go?"

"No. Sit still and keep quiet."

Her tone didn't invite argument so Conryu folded his hands in his lap and watched as she muttered in a language he didn't recognize while waving her hands over the device. A minute later she stopped and touched the grip with one finger. The needle went to 300. She removed her finger and it sank back to 0.

"Grab it again "

Conryu gripped the dowel and the needle immediately snapped back to 10,000. He looked up at the wizard. Her face had twisted into a vicious snarl.

"Sorry."

She snatched the device off the table, muttering about cheap bureaucrats, faulty equipment, and how could she do her job if the junk they gave her didn't Work right. Conryu Wouldn't have dared speak even if he had some idea What Was happening. She dragged a tan satchel out from under the table and started rummaging through it

"Ma'am—"

"Quiet. We're going to have to do this the old-fashioned Way." She pulled out an eighteen-inch length of slim, tapered black Wood. A second later the tip gloWed With a faint light.

"Is that a magic Wand?" Conryu asked.

"Not in the Way you mean. It's a first-generation tester. If it gloWs you can do magic and the brighter it lights up the stronger you are. Same as the first one you tried, but Without the gauge so it's less precise. Hopefully it's also less apt to break. Take it."

He took the Wand and it immediately burst into a blinding gloW. He clamped his eyes shut.

"Drop it!"

The Wand clattered to the hard tabletop and the light Went out at once. The Wizard stared at him With a curious little froWn that made him more uncomfortable than the earlier snarl

"What's going on?" he asked in honest confusion. "Everyone knoWs boys can't do magic."

"Young man, that's an excellent question. Either there's something Wrong With all my equipment or We have a serious situation. Whichever it is, I can't resolve it here. You and the young ladies are going to have to come With me to the Department of Magic. They have a much more precise unit they'll run you through Can you do me a favor and collect Miss Kane and Miss

16

Morrow? I'll call my superiors and meet you out front You'll see a panel van with the government seal on the side "

"Yes, ma'am " Conryu stood up and left the office in a daze

No way could he do magic There were no male wizards and never had been Something must be wrong with her equipment, nothing else made sense

Jonny jogged up to him "Pizza time "

Conryu looked up, noticing his friend for the first time "What?"

"Dude, you okay? You look like you seen a ghost "

"I'm fine, I think Pizza's going to have to wait The wizard wants to take me, Kimmy, and Maria to the Department of Magic for retesting She thinks there's something wrong with her equipment Want to help me find Kimmy?"

"Sure "

They walked down the all-but-empty hall It looked like everyone had gone home already Conryu hoped Kimmy hadn't left yet He didn't have her cell number and it would be a bitch to have to track her down

They continued on past the empty library and Jonny stopped "Why would they need to test you again?"

Conryu sighed "Because the machine reacted to me The little needle went all the way to 10,000 when I touched it It's got to be broken, but she says they can only straighten it out at the Department "

"That's nuts "

"Tell me about it Why don't we have the office page Kimmy? We could wander the halls for hours and never find her "

"Good call What about Maria?"

Conryu shook his head. "She's waiting out front, remember? Shit! What about my bike?"

Jonny laughed. "With everything that's happened, that's what you're worried about?"

* * *

"What do you mean 'retest'?" Maria asked.

"Yeah!" Kimmy added

They stood beside a blue van with a picture of bronze scales of justice on the side. The plates on the front simply read, GOV. The wizard hadn't joined them yet and the girls were getting antsy. Not that Conryu blamed them. He wasn't exactly thrilled about things either

It was an hour after noon on what Conryu had hoped would be a short day of school and a long afternoon of tweaking the carbs on his bike. He gazed longingly at the sleek black machine twenty spaces to their right. Maybe the wizard would let him follow along behind her. It wasn't like he planned to run away. He wanted this sorted out as much as anyone.

"I don't know what to tell you. The wizard asked me to find you and bring you here, so I did."

"But why? There had to be some reason she wanted us to take the test over again." Maria eyed him. "You're hiding something "

"What are you doing here at all?" Kimmy asked. "Testing us again makes a little sense, but why you?"

He wracked his brain, but saw no way around telling them. "The machine reacted to me. She didn't know why, but just to be safe she wanted me to be tested again at the office. The wizard seemed to think there was something wrong with her equipment "

The wizard emerged from the main entrance, her satchel slung over one shoulder She raised her hand and the lights flashed on the van "Everybody in "

Conryu pulled open the sliding door so Maria and Kimmy could climb up When the wizard reached them he asked, "Can I follow on my bike? I don't want to leave it here "

"No My boss doesn't want you out of my sight She almost took my head off for sending you to find the girls We've kicked a hornet's nest with this and I'm afraid things will be tricky for a little while "

Conryu shook his head, gave one last look at his bike, and climbed in She'd be okay He had the key and the parking lot was covered by video cameras Besides, how long could a retest take?

"Did you speak to my dad?" Maria asked

In all the excitement Conryu had forgotten Mr Kane was the number three man in the Division of Magic and the city chief They had always gotten along well Maybe he'd be able to get Conryu out of this mess

"Not directly " The wizard started the van and pulled out of her space "But I'm sure word will reach him soon enough "

"I should call my mom " Conryu fished his cellphone out of his pocket

"No calls until after the retest " The wizard pulled out onto the highway and turned toward the city center "Just be patient This shouldn't take any time at all "

Maria took his hand, whether to comfort him or herself he couldn't say and didn't care. He felt better at once.

"Don't worry. Dad will let your mom know what's happening. She's only one building over after all."

"Mom was working from home today, but I'm sure you're right. He'll let her know." Conryu shook his head and laughed. "And I thought the only excitement we had to look forward to was the carnival this weekend."

"Hey," Kimmy said. "What about me? My parents don't work for the government or have anyone to contact them."

"Everybody relax," the wizard said. "My boss will take care of everything and have you guys home in time for supper."

They spent the rest of the trip to the city center sitting quietly, each lost in their own thoughts. The van finally stopped in front of a stone-and-steel building with a giant iron pentagram hanging three stories up. They all piled out and gathered in front of the van.

The Department of Magic was one of four buildings all connected by enclosed walkways. To the left was the Science Department, where Conryu's mother worked. To the right was the sector seat that housed courts, the DMV, and a variety of other small bureaucracies, far more than Conryu cared to keep track of. The final building held the security force headquarters. The only difference between the four buildings from the outside was the symbol hanging from the facades.

"Come on, come on, everyone's waiting." The wizard hustled them toward a bank of doors.

Conryu did a quickstep and held the door for the ladies. When everyone had passed by he followed, letting the door close behind him. A tingle ran through him as he stepped past the

20

wards The magic wouldn't allow anyone to enter if they carried weapons The spell was much more efficient than metal detectors

The lobby consisted of an open area with polished stone floors, bland artwork on the walls, and three secretaries behind a bank of windows Four halls branched left and right leading deeper into the building Their guide showed no hesitation, taking the second on the left

"Where are we going?" Kimmy asked

The wizard glanced back, but didn't break stride "To the primary testing machine It's enchanted with permanent runes and tied to the building's defensive wards There's no way it'll give a false reading "

"What does it mean if we get the same results here?" Conryu asked

She shook her head "That problem's above my pay grade Soon as I deliver you, you're someone else's problem "

Conryu appreciated her honesty if not her compassion The wizard finally stopped in front of a door labeled Testing Department She knocked once and pushed the door open

Four people waited inside, three standing, one pacing The only one Conryu recognized was Mr Kane He had a salt-and-pepper goatee and sharp brown eyes They had all gathered around a steel-and-ceramic cylinder Two handles protruded from the rune-covered device below a digital readout It looked way more impressive than the flimsy wooden thing they'd given the wizard

"Dad!" Maria ran over and hugged her father She barely came to his shoulder "What's going on?"

"I'm not certain yet, sweetheart Conryu "

Conryu went over and shook his hand. "Mr. Kane. Did you call my mom? What's going to happen?"

"Take it easy, son. Connie's on her way and she said she'd fill your father in." Mr. Kane turned his gaze on Kimmy. "I contacted your parents as well, Miss Morrow. They'll be here as soon as they can"

"Thank you, sir." Kimmy's whole body visibly relaxed.

"We may as well start the retest. Thank you for bringing the kids in, Mercia," said one of the other occupants of the room, an older woman whose bright blue eyes were surrounded by fine wrinkles. Her graying blond hair seemed to meld with her matching gray government-issue robe

The wizard began touching a series of runes on the device, causing them to light up. When she finished she grasped both handles and the digital readout said 1,376. She nodded once, seeming satisfied.

"Excellent idea, Terra, thank you," Mr. Kane said. "Would you like to go first, Maria?"

"I'll just get out of your hair," Mercia said.

"No one's going anywhere until this matter is settled." A hard-eyed man in a red-and-gray security service uniform moved to block the door.

"It'll be okay." Mr. Kane patted Mercia on the shoulder and guided the wizard to an empty chair in the corner of the room. He turned back to Maria. "Go ahead, sweetheart."

Maria walked over and grasped the handles. A few seconds later 1,943 appeared on the readout.

Terra consulted a notebook she'd removed from her robe. "Your original result was 1,950 so this is well within the margin of error for the portable device. Miss Morrow, if you please."

Kimmy switched places with Maria and touched the machine. Her result was 953.

Terra nodded. "Good, also well within the margin of error. Mr Koda, your turn."

Conryu took a breath, said a silent prayer for zero, and grasped the handles. Three seconds later the readout read 12,756. Stunned silence filled the room. Conryu couldn't take his eyes off the display. How could this be happening to him?

Finally Mr. Kane said, "I thought you only pulled 10,000 on the portable device?"

"The portable tester only goes to 10,000," Terra said before Conryu could gather his thoughts. The blond wizard looked at him, her eyes shining. "I'm looking forward to determining how you can exist, Mr. Koda."

Good thing someone was looking forward to it, because he sure as hell wasn't.

* * *

The Department wizards and Mr. Kane huddled up in a little conference as far from Conryu and the girls as possible given the size of the room. For five minutes they talked in low voices, totally ignoring the subject of their deliberations, that is to say, him.

Finally the last member of the gathering said, "He can't be human."

She was an attractive woman in her late thirties with pixie-cut brown hair and eyes so dark they almost looked black. The wizard dressed in the familiar gray robe of a government wizard though unlike the others hers had a small badge with a scale on it.

Conryu moved aWay from the machine and stared at her. "Say What?"

The door to the little room burst open, nearly flattening the man in red as Conryu's mother came running in. She rushed over, hugged him, then patted him all over looking for injuries. Just What did she think these people had done to him?

"Mom, relax, I'm fine. Where's Dad?"

"At the dojo, Where else? He says he's sure you'll be okay and he'll see you at supper." She turned to Mr. Kane. "What's going on, Orin?"

"That's exactly What We're trying to figure out. It appears Conryu has Wizard potential and We're trying to determine hoW that can be."

Conryu's mother stared at him as if seeing him for the first time. "He's a boy. Boys can't be Wizards."

The Wizard that had been speaking before his mother burst into the room cleared her throat. "As I Was saying, Mr. Koda must have some non-human blood in him, probably demon, probably from long ago. Like a recessive gene, it's come to the surface after many dormant generations"

"Conryu doesn't have any demon blood." They all turned to find Mrs. Kane standing in the doorWay. She'd traded her kimono for a sharp black pantsuit. "If he did he Wouldn't be able to live in a building protected by my Wards. He's as human as you or I."

"Shizuku." The government Wizard's lip curled in an ugly sneer When she spoke. Definitely some history there. "If it Was thin enough I'm sure he could slip past your Wards."

"No, Clair, not even a drop of demon blood could get past"

24

The two women stared at each other like angry cats Conryu's head spun and he couldn't stop thinking that if anyone else showed up they'd need a bigger room

"Clair, Shizuku, please" Mr Kane raised his hands in a placating gesture "The test is simple enough, assuming Conryu is willing to let us take a little blood"

Everyone stared at him "Yeah, sure, help yourself"

"You don't have to do this, Conryu," his mother said With her pale and drawn face she looked as worried as he felt

"Yeah, I do At this point, I'm a little curious to see if I'm human or not I'm not sure what's worse, that I have demon blood or I'm a wizard Either one makes me a freak"

Maria ran over and hugged him "You're not a freak and we all love you no matter how the test turns out"

"Thanks," he whispered in her ear

Terra raised a narrow strip of yellow paper and a needle "Ready?"

Conryu gently moved Maria aside and held out his trembling right hand

Terra poked his finger and caught a drop of blood on the paper "If it turns black you have demon blood, white angel blood, and blue elf blood"

They all stared as the seconds ticked by Nothing happened After a full minute Terra flipped the paper into a trash bin "He's human, Chief"

"That's a relief," Conryu said

"Actually it isn't" Mr Kane scrubbed his face with one hand

"It isn't?" Conryu asked

"No. If you were a human with demon blood and some powerful if limited magical powers, that would fall well within our range of experience. Unusual, but nothing to get worked up about. On the other hand an ordinary, fully human male, with the most powerful magical potential ever recorded..." Mr. Kane shook his head. "Not only is that something the entire world would say was impossible, it totally rewrites everything we thought we knew about wizardry. You, my young friend, are about to cause me a giant headache. When word of this gets out..."

"Aren't we overlooking an obvious explanation?" Clair said. "Maybe our testing device is also malfunctioning."

Mrs. Kane sighed and walked over to the machine. She grabbed the handles and 1,926 appeared on the screen. "If you check your records you'll see the power level is the same as my last test. Clair?"

Clair glared at Mrs. Kane then took her place in front of the machine. 1,754. "Mine is the same as well."

"As was mine," Terra said. "The machine is functioning properly. We simply need to accept the reality that Conryu Koda has the potential to be a wizard and that we may never know why."

The wizards and non-wizards began muttering amongst themselves. Conryu didn't know what to think, but it seemed pretty clear his fate was being quietly decided for him.

He raised a tentative hand. "Excuse me. The thing is, I'm not interested in being a wizard. Can't we just forget this ever happened?"

"I'm sorry, Conryu." Mr. Kane laid a hand on his shoulder. "But the law is very clear. Anyone with the potential to be a wizard

26

must be trained at the academy The penalties for failing to do so are quite severe for you and anyone that helps you avoid going."

"Why?"

Mr. Kane sighed. "Let's take a walk, Conryu."

"Orin!" his mother said.

"Sir, I'm not sure that's a good idea," the security man added

"Adam, Connie, calm down. I think our young friend needs some fresh air. God knows I do."

Mr. Kane guided him out of the stuffy lab and into the cool hall. Conryu gulped huge lungfuls of the fresh air. "Thanks. If I didn't get out of there soon I was going to lose it."

"I had a hunch. I'm sorry this has all fallen on you so suddenly. I know you had plans."

"I still have plans."

Mr. Kane shook his head. "Whatever they were, your plans are gone. In the fall you'll be on the train to the academy with the other young wizards. The sooner you accept that the better off you'll be."

Conryu couldn't believe what he was hearing. "I've known what I wanted to do since I was twelve and first entered Mr. McShane's bike shop. Now you're telling me I have to give up my dreams?"

"You don't have to give them up, but you do need to delay them by four years. Once you've completed your training there's nothing that says you have to work as a wizard." Mr. Kane scratched his bald head. "I've never heard of a wizard that did some other type of work since wizards can make fantastic money, the strong ones anyway. My point is you need to accept that for the next four years your plans are on hold. You've got all summer to make peace With it."

Conryu clenched his jaW and badly Wanted to hit something. "What's the big deal anyWay? It's not like I can even use magic as I am noW. Why not just leave me like this?"

"HoW do you like your truth, ugly or gentle?"

"Ugly. Nothing about this day has been attractive since I touched that Woman's toy back at school."

"Okay, here it is. The state regards Wizards as indispensable assets. In a time of crisis the more Wizards We have to call on the better our nation's chance of survival. Even one Wizard, especially one as poWerful as you Will become, might be the difference betWeen Winning and losing a War."

"So I'm just a Weapon in the government's arsenal?"

Mr. Kane shrugged. "You said you Wanted it ugly."

* * *

Orin had sent the kids and their parents home and led Adam and Terra from the cramped testing lab to a more spacious conference room. Clair had remained behind to check the testing equipment one more time. He doubted she'd find anything, but better safe than sorry. The door had barely closed When Adam and Terra started going back and forth about the best Way to handle the revelation about Conryu

He felt bad for the kid. Conryu Was a good boy, and he hated to yank the rug out from under him all of a sudden, but the laW Was clear. Not to mention if he achieved even half his potential he'd end up as the most poWerful Wizard in recorded history. Orin couldn't simply throW aWay that sort of resource.

As the argument continued Orin only listened with half an ear He leaned on the windowsill and stared out over the city Everything looked exactly the same as it did yesterday Same skyline, same floating island, same everything Nothing to indicate that the whole world had changed

"We can't let word of this escape " Adam slammed his fist on the conference room table, drawing him back to current debate "We'll institute a total intelligence blackout Keep it totally quiet, send him to the academy by special flight "

"That's exactly the wrong thing to do," Terra said "At some point the media will find out about Conryu's existence When they do we'll be accused of a cover up which will make everything worse We need to have a press conference and announce that a male wizard has been discovered We don't need to provide details, but we do need to get out in front of the situation "

"Chief?" He turned to find Adam looking at him, hands on hips "It's your decision What are we going to do?"

"If there's one thing I've learned after fifteen years in government it's this: a cover up is always a bad idea, except for national security issues We'll schedule a press conference for tomorrow afternoon No questions, just a brief announcement "

"The boy will have to be there," Terra said

Orin nodded Conryu wouldn't be thrilled, but she was right, he had to be there Orin seldom had to ruin someone's life and the fact that it was a young man he thought of like his own son made it even worse He needed an antacid from the bottle in his desk

The conference room door flew open and an old man with wild white hair wearing a tan cardigan and black pants rushed in "Where is he? Where's the boy wizard?"

29

Orin groaned. Just when he thought the day couldn't get any worse. Leave it to Professor Angus McDoogle to make a liar out of him. "I sent him home, Angus. Conryu's had a long, exhausting day."

"You sent him home without introducing me? That boy is the key to proving my theory."

"Your theory is garbage, Angus," Terra said. "Conryu isn't going to change that "

"It is not garbage." The old professor's face turned bright red. "Despite what those narrow-minded fools at the Glasgow Institute might say. The Aegis of Merlin is a perfectly reasonable hypothesis "

Terra shook her head. "You think the idea that Merlin was not only real, but that his spirit is watching over and protecting humanity is a reasonable theory?"

"I do and it is. When everyone said my theory was impossible what did they claim as the primary reason? That men couldn't be wizards. Well, this boy puts the lie to that argument. If one young man has the potential to be a wizard then there's no reason another one couldn't have become a wizard fifteen hundred years ago "

"Even if I grant you that another male wizard existed and served as the basis for the Merlin legend, that in no way proves his spirit somehow lingered beyond death to watch over the world."

"Stay a skeptic if you wish." Angus tried to smooth his white hair to no effect. "Now that I've got evidence to support the first half of my theory, it's only a matter of time before I prove the rest of it "

Terra drew a breath to launch into another argument, but Orin cut in. "You two can continue this argument on your own time. What we need to focus on now is Conryu. It's up to us to make this transition as smooth and painless for him as possible. I'll send word to some reporters I know and set it up for three tomorrow. Adam, see about security for the press conference. We'll have it outside in front of headquarters so we can retreat directly back inside when we're finished."

Adam nodded and left the room to begin.

"What about me?" Terra asked.

"Try to think up some reasonable ideas for why a male wizard might have turned up after all this time. We can't just drop a fact like that on the world without offering some sort of explanation."

"I'll get Clair to help."

"Are you sure? She has certain political leanings that may make this difficult for her."

Terra stood up. "Just because Clair was a member of the Le Fay Sorority at the academy when she was young doesn't make her sympathetic now. She's a professional. I'm sure she can set any personal feelings aside and do her job."

"Fine, but keep an eye on her."

Terra took her leave and Orin found himself alone with Angus. The bright-eyed Scotsman closed the distance between them. "When can I meet him?"

"I'll introduce you tomorrow, before the press conference." Angus grinned, prompting Orin to raise a threatening finger. "But only if you promise to stay on your best behavior. I won't have you harassing that boy or turning him into the poster child for your pet theory"

"But—"

"No buts. You put so much as a toe out of line and I'll see you transferred to the most remote outpost I can find. Clear?"

31

"Of course." Angus spun on his heel and stalked out.

Orin Watched Angus until the door closed behind him. Why did the crazy professor have to end up at his department? Orin's lips curled in a bitter smile and he rubbed his throbbing temples. Was it bad luck or the spirit of Merlin?

Chapter 2

Press Conference

L ady Raven quietly digested the news that a male wizard had been found She sat on the edge of her soft couch in the richly appointed apartment she used when she needed privacy Illusion magic blocked out the last annoying shafts of sunlight, leaving her with nothing but the dim, red glow from a pair of drift lights Though the magic blocked the light she could still look through the window at her city The Hierarchs had assigned Sentinel City to her because they trusted her to oversee the great task

A light floral incense burned in an infuser, filling the room with a pleasant scent Both the light and the smell served to settle her nerves and enhance her focus If ever Lady Raven needed to focus, it was now

The impossible thing the Le Fay Society feared most had come to pass To think she'd live to see a male wizard born It was impossible, yet she'd seen the test results with her own eyes She could scream, rail at the gods, or deny to her heart's content, but it wouldn't change the essential truth

The boy existed, and in her city no less. That made it Lady Raven's responsibility to deal with him. Such an abomination couldn't be allowed to survive. It wasn't natural. In fact he was an insult to the natural order

No man had the wit or grace to wield magic safely. All they were good for was brute labor and producing the next generation. If not for the latter necessity she would have wiped them all off the face of the earth without a second thought. Lady Raven pitied the poor women forced to endure their crude touch. She would happily cut her own throat before she let any man lay a hand on her bare flesh.

She stood up and paced, unable to focus despite her efforts. Plans needed to be made and Conryu Koda needed to die. Luckily Lady Raven had made allies for just such an eventuality. Not that she ever imagined needing to kill a male wizard, but the zealots would be happy to kill any wizard, including her, if they learned who she really was.

Lady Raven laughed and went to her casting chamber. The witless males would never guess the truth. She'd never even met them except on an encrypted online forum. It sickened her to think how many of the psychopaths wandered her city, but a good craftsman used the tools at her disposal

The casting chamber held even less decoration than the almost-empty living room. No windows to offer distraction, no comfortable seats that might lessen her focus. All she had was a simple wooden desk and hard-backed chair. On the far wall a full-length mirror hung in a black, rune-scribed frame.

Lady Raven frowned at her reflection. When had she gotten so old? It seemed only months ago she'd been young and beautiful She snorted at her useless thoughts Who wouldn't trade youth and beauty for knowledge and power? Besides, looks were easy enough to fix

She chanted, weaving words of water and light to shape an illusion around her wrinkled body Her face smoothed and lifted, lips plumped, and teeth cast off their yellow stain When the spell concluded, the youthful face of her favorite persona stared back Once she changed into an appropriate outfit, men would stare as she walked past, drooling like the dogs they were Though she cared nothing for their opinions, Lady Raven enjoyed the power her new look gave her over the weak-willed fools

Ten minutes later Lady Raven stood in front of her apartment building dressed in a short skirt, torn stockings, and half-buttoned blouse With her magically enhanced figure and revealing outfit it didn't take long to flag down a taxi to take her to this persona's so-called job

When they arrived at the internet cafe Lady Raven paid the cabbie and climbed out The cafe occupied an old, run-down building that drew so much electricity through its under-maintained electrical box it was a wonder the place hadn't burned down long before now Not that she had any intention of letting anything happen to the place until she'd finished with it

"You're late, Lacy!" a fat thug said, playing his part as her obnoxious boss to perfection

She'd told the man when she hired him to shout at her and run her down at regular intervals and he seemed to take a certain joy in the task Once he'd dared to lay a hand on her and that offense had earned him a lesson in pain he'd never forget It certainly hadn't happened again

"Sorry, boss," she said

Lady Raven rushed down between two rows of tables, each supporting four computers. They had a good crowd tonight, only three empty stations. Most of the men—it was always men in the cafe—were staring at cavorting nude figures and touching themselves under the tables. It disgusted her, but she expected no better from them

She slipped into the back room where the routers and servers sat in their racks and shut the door behind her. Her laptop rested, closed, on her tiny station. It whirred to life when she opened the lid. When it finished booting up she activated a program that would disguise her current location and logged in to a private chat room where her dupes liked to hang out and talk tough

As usual, the vitriol directed at women in general and wizards in particular on the site was truly horrific. If they didn't have a part to play in her plans, Lady Raven would have been thrilled to murder them all

It took a bit of searching, but she finally found one of her pet zealots. She struck up a conversation, playing the part of a wizard-hating true believer. After a bit of back and forth using particular phrases that established they were who they claimed Lady Raven tossed out the bait, mentioning a rumor of a male wizard.

Disbelief greeted her pronouncement No surprise there She insisted it was true and the idiot argued that it was impossible. They went back and forth some more before Lady Raven said there was going to be a press conference at the Department and if he wasn't a gutless coward he'd be there to kill the abomination.

She logged out and smiled a self-satisfied smile Nothing motivated the idiots like questioning their courage Her tool would show up tomorrow, no doubt about it

* * *

Conryu's fist hammered into the quarter-inch rope wrapped around the wooden training dummy Like a machine gun his palms and forearms smacked the wooden dowels that jutted from it at odd angles His shin slammed into the fake leg with enough force to crack it Sweat dripped off his nose and soaked his hair

He'd come to the dojo early, both to help Dad with the morning class and to take his mind off the press conference Mr Kane had set up for this afternoon So far neither correcting the basic poses of the beginners or pounding out his frustrations on the dummy had done the least bit of good

Mr Kane had stopped by late the night before to tell them what he'd decided, just like Conryu had no say in the matter At least they didn't expect him to speak All they wanted him to do was stand there while the reporters snapped some pictures, like he was some new sort of animal being delivered to the zoo

He hit the center of the dummy with a double palm strike, rattling it in its frame

"Your form is a mess "

Conryu turned toward his father's deep voice The master of the dojo knelt before a small shrine that held a katana and wakizashi set that family legend claimed one of Conryu's ancestors had wielded during the Elf War He didn't know if that was true, but the swords certainly looked old enough with their scuffed black scabbards and frayed ray-skin hilts They were the oldest Weapons in a room lined With just about every type of hand Weapon imaginable, from simple staves to sWords.

"Just trying to Work off some stress."

"Violence Won't help your anger, they feed on each other. Take deep breaths, move sloWly. Let your chi floW from your core to your limbs, carrying the negative emotions aWay."

Dad hopped to his feet and began the familiar kata. Like a man moving in Water his father shifted from one pose to the next, each movement accompanied by deep breathing. Conryu joined in, falling into the rhythm of movements he'd first learned as a four-year-old

As usual Dad Was right. With each shift a little more anger left him until they stopped and Conryu felt at ease once more They faced each other and he looked into the Warm, gentle eyes of his father. Deep and broWn, framed by fine Wrinkles, those eyes held depths Conryu doubted he'd ever plumb.

"Better?"

"Yeah. Thanks, Dad."

They boWed to each other and his father finally smiled. "May as Well enjoy your five minutes of fame, Conryu. In a Week they'll have forgotten all about you."

"I hope you're right."

"Of course I'm right. With age comes Wisdom."

"And humility."

"Smart ass. When are you supposed to head over?"

Conryu yaWned. "Mr. Kane's supposed to pick me and Mom up at tWo."

"You'd better take a shoWer and head home. Can't have you smelling like a dojo on your big day." Dad sniffed and pulled a face. "Though it might convince the reporters to keep their distance "

"Thanks. You coming to the show?"

"Sorry, I have an afternoon class. I'm sure you'll do fine."

Conryu nodded, not at all surprised that his father didn't plan to join them. Outside the dojo Dad didn't like dealing with people. Conryu didn't know why, but Dad seldom went anywhere besides home and to the dojo.

He headed to the locker room while his father returned to meditating in front of the shrine. Conryu took a shower and swapped his sweaty black gi for jeans and a t-shirt. He checked his phone. Only twelve thirty; he had time to stop by the garage on his way home. He had to tell Mr. McShane that he wouldn't be coming to work for him as soon as he'd first hoped. It seemed only right to tell him in person rather than letting him hear it on the news tonight.

Conryu paused to dry a drop of water from his forehead with the bottom of his shirt then slipped out the side door into the alley between the dojo and the pawn shop next door. A car whizzed by as he walked to the end of the alley and turned up the street to the shop. He stopped to look in one of the pawn shop's windows. He'd found some valuable parts over the years, but alas not today. A shiny red electric guitar in the display caught his eye.

He'd never learned to play—too busy with martial arts—but he'd always wanted to. It seemed a funny thing for someone that hated attention to be interested in, but there you go

It only took five minutes to walk from the dojo to the garage Conryu centered himself as he approached the familiar two-bay structure. The right-hand door stood open and a huge gut covered in bib overalls stuck out from under a lift holding a sleek, green racing bike imported from the Empire. The rapid-fire click of a ratchet mingled With the acrid stink of spilled gas. Conryu sighed. What a great place.

"Mr. McShane?"

The ratchet fell silent and the gut jiggled as the master mechanic Worked himself out from under the lift. A kind, grease-smeared face gradually appeared. The handlebar mustache tWitched tWice folloWed by an explosive sneeze.

"Conryu, my boy. Come to give this old man a hand?"

"Don't I Wish. Unfortunately, I have bad neWs."

Mr. McShane heaved himself to his feet. "Your folks are okay, aren't they?"

"They're fine, it's nothing like that. It's just I Won't be able to come Work for you as soon as I Was hoping." Conryu quickly filled him in on the gist of the situation. Mr. McShane listened in silence, his only reaction a slight Widening of his eyes. It Was nice to find someone besides Dad that didn't freak out the moment they heard. "AnyWay, I have to graduate from the academy before I can move on to get my mechanic's license. There's going to be an announcement today, but I Wanted to tell you myself."

"I appreciate that. Don't Worry. Sooner or later there'll be a place for you here Whenever you Want it."

"Thanks." They shook hands and a Weight lifted from Conryu's chest. He really didn't have to give up on his plans. If he Was patient he could still do everything he Wanted to. That thought buoyed him all the Way to the press conference.

* * *

40

Conryu tugged at the itchy collar of the stiff shirt his mother had presented him with upon his return home. She must have gone shopping since he knew for a fact he didn't have anything in his closet this uncomfortable. At least she'd let him wear jeans, a brand new, stiff pair, but he'd take what he could get at this point

The two of them stood together in the entry hall of the Department of Magic. The secretaries were gone and the building silent. No one had even bothered to turn the lights on. All they had to see by was the diffused sunlight from the ceiling windows and what came in through the doors.

Across the road four panel trucks with satellite dishes on their roofs had gathered along with a collection of reporters and cameramen. A hasty platform had been erected just outside the main entrance. Since it was a Saturday the traffic was minimal, nonetheless eight men in security service uniforms had gathered at either end of the driveway to keep confused visitors from entering the area. It was quite a circus, and all for him. Who'd have thought?

"I wish Maria was here."

"I know." His mother patted him on the back. "Orin didn't want to confuse things by having a second student on the platform. Don't worry, in another hour we'll be back home and this will be nothing but a memory."

"Connie, Conryu, there's someone I'd like you to meet."

They turned to find Mr. Kane approaching along with an old man who looked like a mad scientist from a horror movie. He had a bright, not quite sane gleam in his eye. He stared at Conryu with an intensity that Conryu usually reserved for the latest model of motorcycle, the ones with bikini models lying across them. Sweat beaded up on Conryu's back and he forced himself to relax. If Mr. Kane knew the man he couldn't be dangerous.

Mr. Kane gestured to the stranger. "This is Professor Angus McDoogle. He's a visiting scholar from Scotland. He has a hypothesis that you might not be the first male wizard."

The professor rushed over and grasped Conryu's hand in his clammy fingers. "An absolute pleasure to meet you, my boy. Your appearance will be a boon to my work. I hope the two of us can be friends."

Conryu reclaimed his hand and wiped it on his pant leg. "Yeah. So if I'm not the first male wizard, who was?"

"Merlin."

Conryu raised an eyebrow. "Like from the movies? King Arthur's advisor?"

"Not exactly. The Merlin you're familiar with is based on old legends which in turn are potentially based on a real person. I'm still searching for definitive evidence, but you at least prove that a male wizard is more than just a fantasy. I also believe the great wizard's spirit has lingered after his death to influence our world. I will be forever in your debt for proving part of my theory."

What a nut job.

"Um, you're welcome?"

"Okay, Professor." Mr. Kane grabbed the crazy man by the shoulders and turned back toward the interior of the building. "Why don't you head back to your office? We need to begin the press conference."

Angus shrugged off Mr Kane's grip "Surely you'll want to have the world's leading expert on male wizards out there with you to answer any questions the reporters might throw your way "

Leading expert? This guy thought a make-believe character was a real person Conryu didn't know which part of Scotland the professor came from, but they ought to send him back Preferably in a straight jacket

"Angus, we talked about this " Mr Kane spoke in the tone he used to use when Conryu and Maria got into something they shouldn't have "Now get back to your office while you still have one "

The professor shuffled off, grumbling

When he'd gone Conryu asked, "Where'd you dig him up?"

"Conryu!" His mother scowled at him

"It's okay, Connie Angus takes a little getting used to He's been overexcited ever since he learned about Conryu You essentially validate half his thesis Try not to take it personally "

"Whatever you say Can we get this over with? This collar's driving me nuts "

Mr Kane laughed and guided them towards the front doors The little group climbed up on the makeshift platform Ten reporters and cameramen milled around in front of them One lonely photographer snapped pictures The blond wizard from yesterday joined them from another direction She carried a folder tucked under her arm

"I trust you came up with something, Terra," Mr Kane said

"Yes, though it's mostly nonsense and jargon Nothing that would convince an actual scholar "

Mr. Kane smiled. "Never underestimate the poWer of nonsense and jargon. It's the grease that keeps the Wheels of government turning"

"I thought money did that," Conryu muttered.

His mother slapped him on the shoulder, but she had a faint smile

Mr Kane stepped up to the podium and raised his hands The assembled reporters fell silent "Ladies and gentlemen, thank you for coming out today. I'll keep my remarks brief and please remember, no questions. The Department of Magic, in the course of our duties, has discovered the World's first confirmed male Wizard."

Silent stares of disbelief greeted this announcement folloWed by a blizzard of questions. Everyone Was shouting at once and Conryu couldn't make out a single Word other than "impossible." Every question seemed to have that Word as an essential component

Mr Kane raised his hands again, this time to considerably less effect. After several minutes of being completely ignored the reporters fell silent once more

"Thank you," Mr. Kane continued. "As I Was saying, We're not taking questions, but When I finish my remarks our leading researcher Will have more information for you. NoW, this remarkable young man beside me..."

He paused as all eyes and cameras turned to focus on Conryu Who offered a feeble Wave.

"This young man is Conryu Koda. Over the course of our standard annual testing the portable deVice indicated he possessed Wizardly potential."

Mr Kane droned on, telling the press everything that happened yesterday Conryu's attention went to the photographer The man had put his camera away and was staring at Conryu with an intensity that made him uncomfortable

Conryu started to point him out to his mother, but the photographer broke eye contact and reached for his gear bag Conryu blew out a breath Just his imagination

The photographer came up with a saw-backed bowie knife and charged the platform

"For the True Face of God!" he screamed as he reached the edge of the platform

Reporters shouted

Cameramen rushed to adjust their target

The lunatic with the knife leapt onto the platform

Conryu stepped in front of his mother

"Die, abomination!" The photographer charged, the knife raised above his head

Conryu stepped in, grabbed his wrist as the knife descended, twisted and yanked him off balance The man's wrist locked and he doubled over Conryu plucked the knife from his opponent's disabled hand and tossed it over beside the podium

Fists hardened by years of training lashed out, pummeling the attacker in the jaw and temple Conryu hit him eight times in two seconds When he finished, the unconscious man slumped to the stage, just as the security men arrived to claim him

Fat lot of help they were

Once again Conryu found himself the center of attention Questions were shouted his way He shot Mr Kane a desperate look

"Ladies and gentlemen," Mr Kane shouted over the questions, "that concludes our press conference. We'll email you copies of our researcher's notes. Good afternoon."

Everyone retreated to the Department building. As soon as they were inside Mom rounded on Mr. Kane. "I thought you said there'd be good security? Conryu might have been killed."

"No way," Conryu said. "That guy had no idea how to properly use a knife."

"What if he'd had a gun?"

Conryu couldn't argue with that.

"I know you're upset, Connie, but please try to keep calm."

"Calm! What if it had been Maria out there? Would you be able to keep calm?"

"I take your point. However, the assailant has been subdued and we're all safe now."

"This assailant. What about the next one? I never should have let you talk me into this. You've made my son a target."

"Mom, relax. We read about these True Face of God guys in school. They want to kill all wizards. The girls are in just as much danger as I am. Besides, they aren't very good at their job. As of six months ago they'd only managed to murder three wizards, and they've been around for like twenty years."

"Am I just supposed to accept the fact that lunatics with knives are hunting you?"

Conryu cocked his head. "Is there some other option?"

* * *

Detective Lin Chang pulled into the parking lot of the Department of Magic. One of the security officers raised her hand to stop him until he flashed his badge. The woman moved

46

aside and waved him toward a mixed group of police and security officers They were all gathered around a beat-up, rusted-out, once tan pickup That had to be the assailant's vehicle

When Lin had gotten word that Conryu had been attacked by a knife-wielding maniac on national tv he'd jumped to get the case It didn't surprise him to learn Conryu had subdued the attacker He attended the Koda dojo and had seen the young man fight He might be seventeen, but Lin would have put him up against just about any two men he knew and be confident of Conryu coming out the winner Lin simply couldn't let someone get away with attacking a brother warrior, it was a matter of honor

He clambered out of his green sedan, attempted to straighten his perpetually wrinkled suit, gave up and ambled over to the gathering "Someone want to tell me what happened?"

One of the red-shirted security officers stepped away from the group "The assailant drew a weapon in the middle of a Department press conference and attempted to stab the victim, Conryu Koda He was subdued and taken into custody "

One of the cops laughed "Subdued? The medic said that kid fractured the nut's skull Be a wonder if he ever wakes up "

Lin turned his gaze on the cop "And where is the assailant now?"

"Ambulance took him to Sentinel Central Hospital Don't worry, Sarge, we told them to put the guy in a secure room and sent two of the boys along to make sure they did it "

Lin smiled when the officer used his nickname He'd served six years in the Alliance military before being discharged with the rank of sergeant "And the victim?"

"We took his statement and got an address, then sent him home"

Lin clapped him on the shoulder. "Good man. We get an ID on the attacker?"

The same security man handed Lin a shoulder bag "This was all he had on him."

Lin took the bag. "Who are you again?"

"Adam Warren, head of security for the Department."

The truck had no tailgate so Lin set the bag in the bed. He dug a pair of rubber gloves out of his pocket, slipped them on, and pulled the bag open. Nothing too exciting inside. Photography accessories, film, lenses, and, hello, a business card. He took the card out and held it by the edges

Smith's Freelance Photography. There was a picture of a black guy in his mid-thirties, a phone number, and an address. "This the attacker?" Lin asked.

Adam shook his head. "Naw, the perp was a white guy."

"Well, well, the plot thickens." Lin dialed the number on his cell, but it went straight to voicemail. He tapped his chin for a moment. "O'Shea!"

One of the officers, a twenty-five-year-old kid with hair so red it almost glowed moved closer. "Sir?"

"Go over to the hospital. I want the assailant fingerprinted as soon as he's secured."

"It's Saturday, sir."

"So it is. We'll make a detective out of you yet."

"I mean the lab's closed on the weekend, sir."

Lin ground his teeth then took several calming breaths, trying to remember what Sensei said about clarity of thought.

"They don't turn the computers off, do they? Scan the prints and run them through the database. Maybe this clown has a record."

"The techs don't like us messing with their computers, sir"

"If I have to tell you to get those prints just once more you're going to be riding a desk for the rest of your exceedingly short career"

"Yes, sir." Officer O'Shea hurried away to a squad car without further debate.

Lin shook his head. What was the world coming to? Was it too much to expect a little initiative? Christ, they had an attempted murder and he was supposed to wait until Monday to start his investigation rather than annoy the techs

"Anything else I can help you with, Detective?" Adam asked.

"Can't think of anything. What's your cell number? If I think of more questions I'll call." Lin entered the security man's number into his contact list. "Thanks."

"My pleasure. I'd appreciate it if you contacted me about any threat to the Department"

Lin nodded. "Will do."

He memorized the address on the attacker's card and returned it to the bag for the crime scene guys to process The photographer's shop was across town and Lin needed to check on the man. If the attacker stole his gear there might be a body waiting for him. He really hoped not. He hated dealing with bodies

* * *

49

Orin massaged the bridge of his nose. What a fiasco. He couldn't blame Connie for being furious With him. Who Would have imagined one of those cultists shoWing up at the press conference?

After seeing Conryu and his mother to their car Orin had retreated to the conference room they'd used the night before to think. He stared out the WindoW and Watched the floating island drift across the city, one of six that constantly circled the globe and had for as long as anyone could remember

He'd often Wondered What let the massive things stay in the air. It obviously involved magic of some sort, but he'd read several reports by Wizards that had made it their life's Work to figure the islands out and after centuries of study they had no more idea hoW the magic Worked than he did. No one could even land on the things. Some sort of impenetrable force field surrounded them

Orin turned aWay from the WindoW. He Was trying to distract himself rather than face the problem in front of him It all boiled doWn to this: HoW had the cultist learned Conryu Would even be at the press conference this morning? Only a handful of people had knoWn ahead of time and before today he had full faith in them, most of them anyWay.

The door opened and Adam entered. He looked as Worn out as Orin felt. Not that the security chief Would find much sympathy after this afternoon

"Well?" Orin asked.

"The cops searched his car and bag Not much there Turns out his press credentials Were fake. The camera he had Was a cheap knockoff. I turned the investigation over to the city police."

Orin nodded. "This was not our finest hour, Adam. If anything had happened to that boy..."

Adam snorted. "That boy didn't look like he needed our protection. He handled that guy better than I could have. Do you know where he trained?"

"You're kidding, right? Conryu is Sho Koda's son. As in Grandmaster Sho Koda, of Koda style kung fu."

Adam rubbed the back of his neck. "Well, that explains it. I assume you realize we have a leak."

"Yes. It shouldn't take us long to figure out who did it. There were only five people who knew Conryu would be there."

"My money's on the professor. That old man's out of his mind "

"Not a chance Conryu represents his best hope for getting his precious theory acknowledged. Angus would cut his own throat before he let any harm come to Conryu. He's the only one I have complete faith had nothing to do with it."

"What about me?"

The door opened admitting Terra. She looked around. "Where's Clair?"

"I didn't call her in," Orin said.

Terra frowned. "You still don't trust her. What does the poor woman have to do to convince you of her loyalty?"

"Funny you should ask." Orin held up his right hand displaying the silver rune-etched ring on his middle finger. He'd grabbed it from the secure room on his way up. "I had nothing to do with the attack on Conryu Koda."

He pulled the ring off and flipped it to Adam.

"A ring of compulsion?" Terra asked in a horrified tone.

"That's right. There's no other Way to be sure." Orin never took his eyes off Adam.

The security chief put the ring on. "I had nothing to do With the attack on Conryu Koda."

Orin nodded and looked at Terra. "Your turn."

"I have no obligation to put that thing on. Only suspected criminals are required to testify With one of those."

"You're right," Orin said. "You have no obligation, nor do I have any obligation to Work With a Wizard I don't fully trust. I can have your transfer ready on Monday"

"You Wouldn't."

"Try me. I'm going to sort this out one Way or another. Even if it means a Whole neW staff."

Terra held out her hand "GIve It to me"

Adam passed the ring over and she slipped it on. "I had nothing to do With the attack on Conryu Koda."

Orin caught the ring When she threW it at him.

"Satisfied, Chief?"

"Yes, thank you. It's not personal, Terra. I had to be sure. Angus is in his office. I'll test him and then Clair on Monday."

"What if neither of them is responsible?" Terra asked.

"Then We have an even bigger problem than I thought."

* * *

Despite the Saturday traffic Lin made it across toWn in under half an hour. He parked in front of a rundoWn, six-story brick apartment building. The fire escape didn't look like it Would hold a toddler, much less a groWn man. Lin Would have to mentIon It to code enforcement on Monday

The ground floor didn't have a storefront so Mr Smith must work out of his home Technically another violation, but not one that could get somebody killed and therefore none of his business

Lin got out and walked around the rear of his car to the main entrance A call box with fifteen names beside buzzers hung on the wall near a locked door with a steel-mesh-reinforced window Lin ran a finger down the list until he reached Smith, Damon Since there were no other Smiths on the list that had to be his photographer The buzzer actually worked when Lin pressed it, but no one replied

Frowning, Lin pressed the buzzer labeled "Superintendent "

"What?" a metallic voice asked

"Sentinel City Police, open up "

A minute of silence passed before a skinny, shirtless white guy sauntered up to the door "Badge?"

Lin showed him "Let me in, please "

"Got a warrant?"

"I don't want to arrest anyone, I'm just curious if there's a body in apartment 3B Supposed to be pretty hot this week I can just wait until you call me if you prefer "

The super punched a button and a buzzer sounded followed by the clunk of the lock opening "Central air's already busted Last thing we need is a body stinking up the place Which apartment did you say?"

"3B, Damon Smith "

"Oh, the shutterbug " The super went back to fetch his keys and Lin followed "Jesus, he's the only guy living here that ain't into drugs or worse You didn't hear that from me "

"Of course not, Mr?"

"Marco."

"Do you know Mr. Smith, Marco?"

"Not well." The super opened his door, reached in, and came out with a ring of carefully labeled keys. Lin caught the sour smell of spilled beer. "Gonna have to take the stairs, elevator's busted too."

"Does anything work in this building?"

Marco grinned. "Just me and a couple hos up on six. Ugly and Uglier I call 'em. Come on."

Lin followed his guide to a flight of steps so decrepit he feared his foot would crash right through them. The skinny little man didn't pay them any mind, stomping up without a care in the world. Lin tiptoed along behind him, sweating from more than the heat, a silent prayer on his lips that the body removed from the building wouldn't be his.

They reached the third floor in one piece and Marco went straight to the door marked with a tarnished bronze B. When the super reached for the door Lin stopped him. It was already two inches ajar.

Marco looked at him and started to speak. Lin held a finger to his lips, pulled his automatic, and motioned him aside. The little man obliged without complaint.

Lin nudged the door open and winced at the rusty screech. He peeked into the main room. A recliner and tv tray sat in front of a flat screen hung on the wall, with a ragged mattress off to one side. No body.

Pistol leading, Lin lunged through the door. A kitchenette was separated from the main room by a waist-high wall. No joy in there either The only door in the place had to lead to the bathroom If he planned to store a body that's where Lin would put it

Two deep breaths to steady his nerves then he toed the door open A body slumped in the tiny shower Black male in his early thirties Nasty head wound Naked except for a soiled pair of boxers His chest rose and fell, slow and steady Not dead, thank god for small favors

Lin holstered his pistol, took out his phone, and dialed dispatch "I need an ambulance at 6678 Greenway Black male, unconscious with a head wound Send the crime scene boys over too "

He listened for a moment "No, he's not bleeding, just unconscious "

Smith groaned

"Look, I need to go Just send them here as quick as you can " Lin hung up and shook his head The weekend crew was nowhere near as efficient as the regular dispatch team

Smith groaned again and his eyes fluttered

"Mr Smith? Can you hear me? I'm with the police You're safe now "

Smith tried to stand up before slumping back down "What happened?"

"I was hoping you could tell me We found your gear and photography equipment at the site of an attempted murder "

"That son of a bitch hit me with something "

"Yes You're lucky, he had a knife on him as well He might just as well have gutted you Did you know the man that did this?"

"Yeah, Mort Call from 2C I passed him on my way out

from time to time. When he knocked I didn't think much of it. My phone rang and when I turned to answer it, he hit me. Next thing I know I've got a cop in my bathroom."

"Better than a mortician. You say the man that attacked you lived in this building. Did you know him well?"

"No. Like I said, I passed him on my way out sometimes. Seemed like a nice guy, friendly, polite, the kind of person you wouldn't look at twice if you saw him in the street."

Lin nodded. "Sounds like our boy. Thanks, Mr. Smith. The ambulance is on its way. Try not to move around too much in case you have more injuries."

Lin left Smith lying in his bathroom and returned to the waiting super. "You heard?"

"Yeah. I suppose you want to go poke around in 2C now."

"Not just yet. For this I will need a warrant. Excuse me while I make a call."

Fortunately, Lin knew the judge on duty this weekend so it wouldn't be a problem getting him to sign a warrant and email it to Lin's phone. Fifteen minutes later a *bing* announced the email's arrival. Lin pulled it up on the little screen, glanced through it, and turned to the super. "Now I want to look through 2C. Here's my warrant."

Marco didn't even glance at it, he just headed back to the stairwell. Another death-defying trip down the rickety steps and they stood in front of a locked door. "You want me to unlock it or would you prefer to kick it in?"

"If I wanted to kick it in do you think I'd have brought you along? You're certainly not here because of your charm."

"Alright, alright, no need to be a dick about it. Just a second." The super flipped through his key ring, finally settling on the correct one. He opened the door and motioned Lin through with a theatrical flourish. "Have at it. I'm heading back to my office. Unless you want to pester any of the other tenants?"

"If I do, I know where to find you."

The super marched off muttering about cops and not in a good way. Lin put the man out of his mind, drew his pistol, and slipped into the room. He didn't expect trouble seeing as how the resident of the unit was in the hospital shackled to a bed, assuming the guys did their jobs right. Still, better safe than sorry.

Unlike Smith's efficiency, Mort's apartment had a proper bedroom. It didn't take a detective to deduce there wasn't a woman in Mr. Call's life. Takeout food containers littered the small kitchen; it seemed he had a taste for tacos. The apartment's sole bookcase was filled from top to bottom with porn: dvds, magazines, comics, you name it. If there was a naked woman on the cover Mort had a sample. Not exactly what you'd expect from a religious zealot. Maybe the True Face of God cult had a lower bar for membership than the official church.

On a cheap desk in the bedroom Lin found an equally cheap laptop. He opened the monitor and the hard drive spun to life. The screensaver appeared and, fingers crossed, Lin tapped the spacebar. The home screen appeared, no password required. It appeared Mr. Call wasn't terribly security conscious. Good for Lin, bad for Mort.

After an hour of browsing through an obscenely large porn collection, Lin finally found something interesting. Last night Mort had visited a website chatroom where he discussed

Wizards and What an affront to God they represented. He found nothing overt about the attack, but Mort and his mystery partner did discuss the press conference and hoW Wrong it Was for the netWorks to give so much coverage to such blasphemy. It ended With Mort promising to give them something more important to coVer

As far as Lin could tell Mort had acted on his oWn With just a little prodding from the other party. The tech guys Would trace the forum, but most of the chatrooms Where the nuts, kooks, and other Weirdoes hung out Were set up to be anonymous. At the very least it didn't appear to be an ongoing conspiracy. He'd have to go over and speak to the Kodas in the morning.

Chapter 3

Shadow Carnival

Lady Raven switched off the tv and considered blasting it to pieces No, that wouldn't do any good Besides, the company that owned her apartment building didn't know she was a wizard and she wanted to keep it that way She hopped off the couch, tossed the remote behind her, and started pacing

They'd actually broken into regular programing to show the news conference live That demonstrated just how big a deal Conryu Koda's existence was She'd realized it as soon as the main testing unit at the Department confirmed his results Lady Raven would see to it that his death became every bit as big a deal

Not that her zealot had helped much What had the world come to when you couldn't trust a grown fanatic to kill a teenager? On the other hand, considering how easily this particular teenager handled a man with a knife, maybe she hadn't chosen the best method to eliminate him Lucky for her she had plenty of other options

She went to the back wall of her casting chamber and muttered a spell. The wall shimmered and she reached through it to remove a sealed coffer. The moment it was clear the wall solidified. Lady Raven ran her finger over the smooth ebony and whispered another spell.

The lid popped open, revealing the flat black gem inside. It looked like a black diamond the size of her thumb knuckle, but in reality it was a magical construct that, under the appropriate circumstances, would open a gate to the netherworld. For someone as skilled in dark magic as Lady Raven it was a simple matter to alter the requirements of the spell.

Simple, but not quick. When she'd finished prepping the spell night had fallen. That actually worked to her advantage. What she needed done was best completed after sunset and by others. The zealots would have nothing to do with her new plan, but her personal enforcers could handle it easily enough.

Lady Raven closed the box and slipped it into the folds of her black robe. The Skulls lived on the far side of town, well away from anything and anyone that might potentially lead back to her.

She left the casting chamber and crossed the living room to the sliding glass door that led to her balcony. The apartment was on the thirtieth floor so the odds of anyone even noticing her were minimal, but she cast an invisibility spell before she stepped outside just to be safe. The breeze whipped her robe around her.

Perfect. The wind spirits were active tonight. That would make the flying spell easier to cast. A minute later Lady Raven was flying across the brightly lit city like her namesake bird.

Instead of flying straight to the Skull's hideout she swung out wide toward the floating island

Even without a spell to perceive magical auras, the power radiating off the mass of earth and stone overwhelmed her The islands had fascinated wizards forever, but no one, not even the founder of the Le Fay Society herself, the great Morgana, had ever penetrated the wards protecting the islands from trespassers What secrets did the islands hold? Lady Raven doubted anyone would ever know

Enough wasting time She had work to do At her mental command the wind carried her west over the city towards the dull, ragged edge where the dregs went to kill each other or fry their brains with the drug of the month

She landed in front of a particularly dismal example of local housing, a rotting, almost ready to collapse two-story shack Lady Raven sent the wind away before an errant gust flattened the place and killed her thugs before she'd finished with them

The invisibility spell faded away as she walked up the cracked, weed-filled path to the front door She rapped on it and waited A few seconds later a belligerent, leather-clad man opened the door The grip of a pistol jutted out from his belt and a red bandana covered his face Whether to disguise his appearance or to ward off the smell of urine and worse that wafted out of the open door Lady Raven couldn't guess

"Good evening, Bloody Where's your master?"

"Mistress Raven Iron Skull's in the kitchen with the guys Numb shot a bunch of rats and we're frying them up There's plenty if you want some "

Lady Raven swallowed the gorge that rose in the back of her throat "I have already dined Take me to him I have a job "

"Yes, Mistress"

Bloody led her through the filth and past bare studs to what served as their kitchen. A barrel with a fire burning in it covered with a grate served as the stove. A cast iron pot filled with oil snapped and bubbled. She didn't move close enough to see the contents.

Iron Skull leapt to his feet when he spotted her, prompting the others to follow suit or make their leader look bad. His black mohawk stood straight up and stiff today. It looked like he'd used some sort of automotive grease on it. His broad-shouldered chest strained his leather jacket to its limits.

"Mistress Raven. What brings you here?"

"I have a task. A simple one, but it will require a bit of finesse."

Iron Skull scratched his head and belched. "Finesse ain't my bag. Bone, you're up."

Where Iron Skull was broad and thick, Bone Skull was thin, almost skeletal, thus his gang name, with slicked back black hair and only a single tattoo. Lady Raven and the slender biker shared a look of mutual distaste. Bone didn't like her and worse, didn't trust her. She had Iron Skull wrapped around her finger, but Bone was far too intelligent for her liking. Lady Raven preferred her tools dull.

She removed the box from her hidden pocket. Sometimes you just dealt with a less than ideal situation.

"That the same as the other ones you had us hide?" Iron Skull asked.

"Similar. I need this hidden on the grounds of the Shadow Carnival tonight."

"Where?" Bone eyed the black box, his lip curled in distaste.

"It doesn't matter as long as it's out of the way." She held out the box to him.

Bone nodded toward the only other small man in the room. "Give it to Numb. The two of us will get the job done."

He definitely didn't trust her. Lady Raven smiled. He also feared her, though he'd never admit such a thing.

She gave the box to a scowling Numb Skull. The moment it settled in his hands she spoke a spell. "There, now you're the only one that can open it Your instructions are simple Find a hidden place, kill someone, doesn't matter who, and drag their body into it. Inside the box you'll find a black gem. Touch the gem to the body and the magic will activate. Leave the box next to the body and go Nothing to it "

Numb looked from her to Iron Skull. "What about dinner? I shot the rats. Don't seem like I ought to miss out on eating them "

"We'll save you some leftovers. You two get a move on."

Bone grabbed Numb by the shoulder and dragged him toward the door. "Come on."

Lady Raven nodded to Iron Skull and followed the other two out. Assuming her tools did their job the boy would die tomorrow.

* * *

Bone and Numb left their bikes two blocks from the park where the carnival had set up. Despite the clear night the thin crescent moon offered little in the way of light. It was perfect for sneaking around, especially since the island blocked most of the moonlight above the carnival The shops that lined the street

63

had closed for the night so they had no trouble finding a spot to pull in. The roar of their choppers Would alert the carnies if they drove the Whole Way and the bitch queen said she Wanted the job done quiet.

Bone didn't especially give a shit What she Wanted, but if they fucked up Iron Skull Would have a fit that might end With one or both of them dead. The leader of their club Wasn't knoWn for his even temper and gentle disposition. Not exactly shocking for someone in their line of Work, but no less dangerous for all that

They dismounted and Numb headed for the park.

"Hold up," Bone said

"What? I Want to get this done and get back before the guys eat all the leftovers "

"Will you forget about the fuckin' rats? That shithole We're livin' in is full of them. You can shoot some more tomorroW. NoW open that box."

Numb pulled the black box out of the satchel of tools he'd brought. "Why do you Want to open it noW? She said We're supposed to leave it With the body."

"Fuck her. Open it."

Numb shrugged and pulled the lid open. Inside Was a matte black gem that didn't reflect the meager light. "What noW?"

"Take the gem and put the box in my saddlebag."

"That's not What she said to do, Bone."

Bone grabbed Numb by the front of his jacket and yanked him close so their noses almost touched Bone might have been skinny, but he Was stronger than he looked. "She ain't here.

Now do what I tell you. And make sure you wrap it in my spare bandana. Last thing I need is to get a curse off the fuckin' thing."

Numb's eyes went wide, as if the idea of a curse never crossed his mind. Since he was an idiot it probably hadn't. Numb did as Bone told him and when he finished asked, "What now?"

"Now we do the bitch's job and split."

They walked down the sidewalk toward the park, side by side, just like they owned the street. Nothing made people suspicious like a person sneaking around.

When they reached the edge of the parking lot Numb stopped. "What are you going to do with the box, Bone?"

"Nothing, right now. But sooner or later that witch is going to fuck us over and when she does I want some leverage. If I threaten to show the cops her box it might make her think twice."

"Iron Skull's not going to like that."

He certainly wasn't. That's why Bone didn't plan on telling him. "The boss has a soft spot for her. I'm trying to save him from himself. Now shut up and focus."

They swung out wide around the parking lot then moved in closer to the fence surrounding the carnival. In the dim light they couldn't make out much beyond the closest stalls. They circled around until they reached a spot behind a large tent

Numb sniffed and sighed. "Too bad we couldn't come back during the day. I smell hotdogs."

Bone shook his head. Fuckin' moron. "Gimme the cutters."

Numb pulled a pair of short-handled bolt cutters from the satchel and in less than a minute Bone had an opening big enough for them to slip through

The carnival grounds Were quiet; no one Was out and about at this time of night. That should make it easy to find a place to hide the stone, but Would they find someone to kill?

The bikers darted from tent to display to shed. They'd have to risk going out into the main part of the carnival if they Wanted to find someone. Bone inched along the side of a food trailer.

"Hey, Bone, look at that." Numb pointed at What looked like an artificial mini-mountain.

"Will you shut up?" Bone looked closer. There Was a faint light coming from the mountain. If someone Was there they could kill tWo birds With one stone.

He grabbed Numb's sleeve and tugged him along across the open space separating the trailer from the mountain. They stopped beside a dart game. There Was an opening in the front of the mountain, that's Where the light Was coming from.

Numb started to move closer, but Bone stopped him. If there Was a light someone had to be inside. The hunters had to stay patient

Soon enough a shadoW moved in the feeble light and a moment later a pudgy Woman in a polka dot dress emerged from the cave. She had a clipboard and no visible Weapon.

She Would do nicely.

"Go get her," Bone said

"Thanks, Bone." Numb dreW his knife and jogged toWard the Woman.

She never kneW What hit her. Numb came up behind her, clamped a hand across her mouth and sWung around, driving his blade into her chest. She tWitched a couple times and Went still. He might be an idiot, but Numb Was a fine killer.

Bone took a quick look around to make sure no one had noticed the ambush. It looked clear. He ran over to Numb. "Let's move her out of sight. There must be a place in there we can hide her body"

Numb grabbed her under the armpits and Bone got her ankles. They lugged her back toward the cave. Too bad they couldn't have found someone skinnier. The bitch weighed a ton.

Once they moved inside, out of sight, Bone dropped her legs and sighed. "No sense lugging her around until we have somewhere to take her. Let's check this dump out."

They walked deeper into the mountain, following a set of narrow train tracks. The mountain was a ride. Pretty elaborate for a piddling operation like this.

"Hey, Bone, a light"

A thin glowing line in the wall beside the tracks drew the two bikers closer. Bone worked his fingers into the gap and yanked. A door opened revealing a small room filled with machinery

"For maintenance, you think?" Numb asked.

"Probably. This should do nicely. We'll dump her body here and seal it back up."

They retraced their steps, grabbed the corpse, and hauled it to the maintenance room Bone dropped his end in a clear area at the rear of the room

"Fuck!"

"What?" Numb stared at him, a worried frown on his face.

"We left her clipboard outside. If anyone notices that they might come looking. I'll grab it. You fire up the magic."

Numb's eyes went wide. "You want me to do it?"

"She gave you the gem. Hurry up. I want to get out of here."

Bone left Numb to his task and retreated toWard Where Numb knifed the Woman. He'd never admit it, but magic made Bone nervous He supposed it made everyone nervous, but it really gave him the shakes.

After a minute of searching he found the dead Woman's clipboard. He bent to pick it up and froze. Voices Were coming from the opposite Way. In the night With his black jacket and jeans Bone should have been all but invisible.

The voices faded and Bone risked looking up. He caught a glimpse of movement heading into the mountain.

"Fuck." Bone sWitched the clipboard to his left hand and pulled his dagger With the other. It Was a Wicked, eighteen-inch, double-bladed beast, With a deep blood groove running doWn the center. The beast Would take care of any problems he ran into.

* * *

Numb Wanted to argue When Bone left him alone With the dead Woman, Which didn't bother him, and the magic stone, Which did, but he'd gone before Numb could Work up the nerve. He kneW he shouldn't be such a coWard, especially in this job. On the other hand a little fear had kept him alive more than once When the other guys got in a killing mood. Those days When the Wrong Word or even a funny look might get you gutted.

Fuck it. Best to just do the job and go before someone shoWed up. He fumbled around in his bag and finally came up With the black stone. It chilled his hand to the marroW. Was there someWhere in particular he should put it? Mistress Raven hadn't said.

He shivered when he thought of the wizard. If ever there was a person to fear it was her. Numb didn't know how Bone found the guts to risk going against her. He'd do just what she said, when she said it. Way safer than plotting against the terrifying woman.

"Hey!"

Numb fumbled the stone and it bounced into the corner of the room. He spun and found two men that looked like twins with matching brown hair and eyes. They wore grease-covered overalls with tools jutting out of the pockets.

"You ain't supposed to be here," the left-hand man said.

"Is that Gerty?" the other brother asked. "What'd you do to her?"

Numb groped for the hilt of his knife and finally dragged it free of the sheath on his belt. Bone would be back soon. He could hold off a pair of mechanics for a minute or two.

The brothers pulled out their heaviest tools, a monkey wrench and a long screwdriver. Not the most wicked weapons, but either one of them could do you in if it hit you in the head

"We'll bash you good for what you done," the guy with the wrench said.

He lunged at Numb who dodged the clumsy blow and opened a long slash in the mechanic's forearm, not deep, but bloody

Numb grinned. These chumps didn't know how to fight. They were just stupid carnies who walked into the wrong place at the wrong time. He could take them. No problem.

"Jobe!"

The brother With the screWdriver leapt at Numb With no thought for defense. Numb's knife drove deep into the man's chest, but his Weight bore the biker to the floor.

Numb struggled to throW the body off.

"You bastard! You killed my brother."

The second guy fell on him. The heavy Wrench crashed into Numb's head and set the room spinning. A second bloW turned out the lights for a moment

When his vision returned Bone Was standing behind the Wrench guy, his big dagger poking out the front of the carnie's chest. Bone tossed the body aside and knelt beside Numb. He reached doWn and Numb flinched When he touched the side of his head

"Don't look good, Numb."

Numb tried to say he'd be okay, but only garbled nonsense came out. That, combined With the Way Bone Was looking at him said he Wouldn't be okay. That look said he Was about to die.

Bone cleaned his dagger on the dead mechanic's overalls and returned to Numb. He held the ugly blade and shook his head. "You can't ride, brother."

Numb tried to argue, but more nonsense emerged His thoughts Were so jumbled he couldn't even form an argument in his oWn mind.

Bone reached for him With the dagger. The razor edge touched his throat and the lights Went out again.

* * *

Bone grimaced as he Watched the last of Numb's blood spill out across the floor. It Was a shame When you had to kill a brother, but he couldn't ride, and that mushy spot on the side of his skull wasn't something they could just sew up. Maybe a hospital could have done something for him, but Bone doubted it. Numb's brain was as pulped as his skull.

The black gem sat on the floor in the corner of the mechanical room. Bone had no intention of touching it. A quick search of the bodies turned up a pair of pliers in one of the brothers' pockets. It opened just wide enough for Bone to pick up the gem and drop it on the woman's chest.

It seemed to melt into her, a black stain that covered her from breasts to hips. Dark sparks shot out and formed lines and squiggly figures. Bone had seen enough.

"So long, brother "

He left the bodies where they lay and fled the room, pausing only long enough to push the door to the hidden room shut. A catch clicked, securing the door so that not even a glimmer of light leaked out. That should satisfy the bitch.

Bone paused at the mouth of the cave. No one was waiting and nothing moved in the unlit carnival. At least the fight hadn't drawn any attention.

He ran back the way they'd come, following the outer fence until he reached the opening. Once he was clear of the carnival grounds Bone slowed to a walk and took his time getting back to the bike. He'd have to call Iron Skull and tell him what happened. He needed one of the guys to come pick up Numb's bike.

Bone had been preparing for this moment for months He knew exactly where he'd hide the box. Maybe he was wrong and the wizard wouldn't betray them. He hoped so, but if she did he'd make damn sure the witch suffered the consequences.

When he finally reached his bike Bone sat down and pulled out his phone. Now the tricky part: breaking the news to Iron Skull in such a way that their unpredictable leader didn't blow up.

"Boss," he said when Iron Skull answered. "Job's done. Yeah, there was a problem. Numb bought it."

Bone held the phone away from his ear while Iron Skull shouted. When his leader fell silent Bone said, "It was just bad luck. A couple carnies showed up while I was out cleaning the kill sight. Numb killed one of them, but the other bashed his head in before he could free his knife. Yeah, I gutted him. The magic stone did its thing. Can you send a couple of the guys over to ride Numb's bike to the dump site?"

Bone gave Iron Skull the address and hung up. It would take at least twenty minutes for the others to arrive, plenty of time to set things up.

Half an hour later when Bloody and Tough showed up he had everything transferred over to Numb's saddlebags. Numb getting himself killed made his plan much simpler to put into motion. Bone had no idea how he would have explained his missing bike to the guys, but having to hide Numb's made a perfect excuse.

Tough climbed down from behind Bloody who roared off back to the house without a word.

"So what happened?" Tough asked.

Bone gave him the condensed version, leaving out the bit about cutting Numb's throat himself. "We'll drop his bike at the storage site down by the docks."

Tough nodded, not offering so much as a word of argument. Unless fighting and killing were involved Tough generally didn't have many opinions That's what made him so valuable, especially at times like this

The two bikers roared off to the east A small part of Bone almost wished the wizard would betray them just so she'd see what it felt like to have someone beat her

* * *

Mom stood in front of the apartment door with her arms crossed "You can't go "

"Why not?" Conryu had thrown on his comfortable, frayed jeans, shapeless t-shirt, and boots with the intention of heading out to the Shadow Carnival A few hours without having to think about wizards and politics was way up on his to-do list

Ten had just come and gone It was the last day of the carnival and he needed to go if he didn't want to miss it He was supposed to grab Maria and then they were going to meet up with Jonny and Rin

"Why not? You were almost murdered yesterday!"

"Come on I can't stay in the apartment for the rest of my life There'll be hundreds of people there No one would be dumb enough to try something with that many people around "

"Did that man yesterday strike you as the rational sort? Sho, say something "

Dad was sitting in his robe at the kitchen table reading the paper Conryu's face covered half the front page He gave it a shake and looked back over his shoulder toward them "Connie, he has a point Conryu can't hide in here forever If he wants to go, let him go "

Conryu grinned, but his mother didn't budge

When the doorbell rang she jumped a foot off the floor. "Who could that be?"

"It's probably Maria, Wondering Where I am."

Mom looked out the peephole. "I don't knoW him."

"Let me see." Conryu stepped up to the hole and looked out. "It's Detective Chang."

Conryu opened the door Lin Chang stood in the hall Wearing his usual rumpled blue suit and scuffed shoes. Thick, black eyebroWs Went up When he saW Conryu.

"What brings you here, Sarge?"

"Business. Can I come in?"

Conryu stepped aside so the detective could come in out of the hall. He spotted Dad in the kitchen and boWed. "Sensei, Mrs. Kane. I've been assigned to investigate the man that attacked Conryu yesterday. I can't share many details, but I Wanted you to knoW, from our preliminary efforts, he appears to have acted alone, egged on by others in his online community. We see no ongoing threat to your son. Conryu just had the misfortune to draW the attention of a disturbed individual."

"See, Mom? No ongoing threat."

She sighed. "Fine, you can go. But for heaven's sake be careful. And bring me back a bag of caramel corn."

"Will do." Never one to question his good fortune, Conryu reached for the door before she changed her mind

He took the elevator upstairs and found Maria Waiting out in the hall for him. She had on a cute black dress With a scoop neck, silver necklace and bracelets, and White sneakers. Conryu gave her a Wolf Whistle. "You're going to cause a Wreck on the highWay."

She swatted him on the shoulder. "What took so long?"

"Mom didn't want to let me go."

Maria winced and they stepped back into the elevator. He hit the button for the garage

"I guess I can't blame her. I saw what happened on the news last night. It was kind of funny. It looked like the cameras terrified you, but the guy with the knife was no big deal."

"I know how to deal with a guy with a knife, I've trained for it. Cameras and reporters?" He shook his head. "Way out of my comfort zone."

The elevator chimed and the doors slid open. Unlike last time, today the garage was almost full. They wove their way through the cars toward his bike.

"Conryu! Conryu Koda!" A slim, nice-looking brunette in a pale blue suit with a cameraman behind her was running his way. He didn't recognize her or which station she worked for, nor did he care. They were all of a piece to him.

He shouldn't have been surprised, especially since Mr. Kane had warned him the press would come calling, but he was. He had hoped maybe they'd take Sunday off, like normal people.

"Shit!"

"Did Dad tell you what to say to them?"

"He said, nothing "

"He didn't offer you any advice?"

"No, his advice was to say nothing. Which was excellent as that's what I planned to do anyway."

They ignored the shouting woman and hurried on to his parking spot. By the time they got their helmets on and mounted the bike the reporter was five feet away and right in their path.

"Kat Gabel, Channel 7 neWs. Just a feW questions." She shoWed no sign of moving. "HoW does it feel to be the first male Wizard?"

Conryu touched the ignition and tWisted the throttle. Without a helmet the roar from the big engine reached an almost deafening volume in the enclosed garage. The Woman froWned and covered her ears. When the engine had died back doWn to an idle she took a breath to try again.

She Was determined, he had to give her that. He tWisted the throttle again, farther this time The volume forced the reporter back a step. Conryu cupped his hand beside his head and shrugged

The reporter shook her head and moved aside, motioning her cameraman to join her. Conryu tapped the side of his helmet With his index finger and roared up the ramp, grinning beneath his helmet

It Was a ten-minute ride to the carnival grounds. The company that ran it set up in one of the city parks not far from the government offices. You could see the Ferris Wheel from a mile aWay. They parked in a field just outside the shadoW and headed toWard the grounds. A temporary fence surrounded the carnival With a single opening, a slanted shack sitting beside the gate. He hoped the carnival company didn't pay Whoever built it too much

They stepped into the shadoW and entered another World. The bright morning sun changed to tWilight. Conryu glanced up, but the bottom of the floating island lay in shadoW so deep he couldn't make out any details.

76

Sunday was always the darker of the two carnival days since the island hung directly over the grounds from dawn to dusk The Ferris wheel looked like it almost brushed the bottom of the island, but that had to be a trick of the light The island flew over skyscrapers, certainly a Ferris wheel would be in no danger of hitting it

"Does it look lower than usual this year?" Maria asked

"I thought it was my imagination It can't be though, can it? I mean the island flew over dozens of buildings to get here It must be a trick of the shadows "

Maria cast a worried look up at the island and shook her head "You must be right Where are we meeting Jonny and Rin?"

"By the snack stands, where else? By the way, you still owe us a pizza "

Maria stopped and dug through her purse She finally came up holding a thick silver ring covered in runes "Mom would have killed me if I forgot to give this to you "

Conryu accepted the band and looked it over It was simple enough, smooth and cool to his touch "Thanks, but what's it for?"

"It's magic Mom enchanted it herself The ring creates a barrier around whoever wears it powerful enough to stop anything short of a point-blank shot with a large caliber bullet It's useless against knives or clubs, something about velocity and deflection I didn't really follow her whole explanation "

If Maria couldn't follow the explanation Conryu didn't even want to try He slipped the ring on and it seemed to shrink a little for a better fit At least it wasn't gaudy And if it worked as well as Maria said, it would be worth wearing "I'll be sure to thank your mom, but don't think you're getting out of buying lunch."

"I just gave you a potentially life-saving magical artifact."

"Yeah, thanks again. I like pepperoni and sausage on my pizza."

"You're horrible."

They resumed walking through the twilight toward the carnival gate. It was definitely darker than last year and it would only get worse the closer they came to the center. Conryu fished a ten out of his wallet and when they reached the little shack handed it to a woman in a clown suit. She stamped their hands with little smiley faces and they went onto the grounds.

"Thanks." Maria got a nostalgic smile when she looked at the stamp.

"Sure. Does your bling do anything?"

"My necklace does the same thing as the ring I gave you and I just thought the bracelets looked pretty."

They walked down a path lined with rip-off games featuring cheap stuffed animals and plastic jewelry. Six people sat in a row, trying to hit a clown's nose with water guns so they could pop a balloon. Conryu grinned when they passed a ring toss game that used glass milk bottles for targets.

"Remember the year you made me spend thirty bucks trying to win you a stuffed cow at the ring toss?"

"Sixth grade. I was in my 'barnyard animals are cute' phase. I thought you were going to strangle that carnie when he tried to talk you into taking the giraffe instead of the cow."

"I could have bought you an actual calf for what I spent on that game. I wasn't going anywhere with a stupid giraffe."

"You were really sweet " They linked arms and continued on

A little past the bumper cars Conryu caught a whiff of frying food Not far now

"Five bucks says Jonny has funnel cake in one hand and a giant soda in the other "

"Double or nothing Rin's trying to steal some "

"You're on "

* * *

Conryu spotted Jonny trying in vain to keep Rin from tearing a chunk out of his funnel cake The pair of them were standing beside a picnic table ten feet from the concession stands They both had on jeans, though Jonny's were torn and Rin's a size too small

Rin reached for another piece and Jonny tried to stop her without spilling a half-gallon soda Conryu glanced at Maria and they both started laughing

When he caught his breath Conryu said, "Do we know our friends or what?"

Maria managed to nod between giggles

"Hey!" Jonny waved them over and in the process moved his snack out of Rin's reach

They all sat around the table Conryu snatched a chunk of funnel cake and ate it before Jonny could complain "What's wrong, Jonny, didn't they have full gallon cups?"

"Give me a break, I'm splurging Saw you on the news last night You really laid that dude out "

Conryu shrugged "He almost kept me from coming today Mom was pretty freaked out Detective Chang stopped by this morning, he pulled the case. Looks like I'm in the clear for now."

"So what's the plan?" Maria asked. "The usual? Too much food, ride the rides, waste some money on games, head home and sleep it off?"

"Works for me." Jonny took a huge bite of cake and almost choked.

"They have a new ride this year," Rin said. "It's called the Haunted Cavern. Sort of a mixture of haunted house and roller coaster. Looks like fun."

"It must be popular," Jonny said when he'd caught his breath. "Damn thing takes up a quarter of the grounds. Bet it took a week to set up and they did it right in the center of the park."

"That's not far from here," Maria said. "Let's check it out."

"I thought it was going to be food then rides," Jonny said.

"You're always hungry." Conryu grinned. "A pound of funnel cake ought to hold you for one ride. It probably only takes five minutes."

"You always take Maria's side."

"That's because I'm always right." Maria flipped her hair over her shoulder

"She's got you there, Jonny," Rin said.

"Okay, okay, I know when I'm beat." Jonny inhaled his food and stood up. "Let's do this."

The four of them walked toward the center of the carnival, Jonny and Rin in the front, Conryu and Maria bringing up the rear. The darkness increased with every step.

Conryu shivered. He knew he wasn't imagining it, the grounds had never gotten this dark before.

Maria grabbed his hand and held it in a death grip "Do you feel it? Something's wrong."

"You mean the chill? I think it's just because so much sun is being blocked."

"It's not a physical chill. It feels like someone walked over my grave "

"What does that mean?" Conryu's gaze darted around, trying to spot whatever was making Maria nervous. In the shadow he couldn't see more than fifteen feet in any direction. The only real light came from the flashing bulbs above a concession stand selling hotdogs and all they did was make the shadows dance.

They'd slowed to a crawl, letting Jonny and Rin pull well ahead

Jonny glanced back. "What's the matter, you two chickening out?"

"Come on, Maria. This ride looks really cool." Rin waved at them to hurry up

Maria huddled against Conryu's chest, her whole body trembling. "We need to go, now."

"Alright." Conryu motioned Jonny and Rin to go on ahead. "Maria's not feeling well. I think I'd better take her home "

Rin rushed back. "What's wrong? You haven't eaten anything yet so it can't be the food."

A deep snarl filled the air and red spots of light appeared behind Jonny and Rin.

"It's too late," Maria murmured.

The shadows swirled around the crimson lights, getting darker and more solid by the second. Half a minute later two hounds as black as a moonless night stood in the middle of the carnival grounds, their eyes gloWing like molten lava.

"Cool special effects," Jonny said.

"They aren't special effects." Maria tugged Conryu back the Way they'd come. "Those are shadoW hounds. Run!"

Conryu and Maria ran back toWard the gate, Rin and Jonny right on their tails. They dodged annoyed visitors When they could and shoved them aside When they couldn't.

Shouts turned to screams When the shadoW hounds let out a roar that Was half bark and half snarl.

"They've fully entered our plane of existence," Maria said.

"Plain English for those of us Whose mother isn't a Wizard," Conryu said betWeen gasps.

He glanced over his shoulder. The hounds Were pounding after them, ignoring all the other patrons Rin had fallen three paces behind Jonny.

The hounds Were only ten feet from her.

"Can I hurt them?" Conryu asked.

"No. They have no substance. They kill by draining the life from you. Only magic can destroy them."

The hounds leapt over Rin and kept on coming.

Just as he feared. They Were after him.

"Jonny, break right, circle around, and help Rin. Get her out of here "

"What about those things?"

"They Want me. I'll draW them off. Help Rin and get out of here "

"No Way, bro. I'm not letting you face those things on your oWn."

"I'm not going to face them, I'm going to run like hell for my bike. Now go."

Jonny scowled, nodded and broke off. The hounds ignored him the same way they did Rin. If Conryu had had any doubts about his theory, that settled it. He turned to Maria.

"Don't even say it." She glared at him.

He grinned despite the danger. That was exactly the reaction he'd expected. "I was going to say, is there any way we can stop them?"

"Not without magic."

Conryu snagged a ketchup bottle off the counter of a food stand, spun, and flung it at the hound behind them. It passed through the monster without slowing it.

Wait, weren't there two hounds?

He turned back just as the second hound emerged from the shadow of a dart game and leapt at them.

Conryu tugged Maria aside. The hound missed them by inches. The chill of its passing froze Conryu to the bone.

He staggered as suddenly cold muscles started to cramp. "How much further?"

"I can see the fence. We're almost there. What are those people doing?"

Conryu looked up. Hundreds of people were milling around in front of the fence.

"Shit!" Maria said.

"What?" Maria never swore. Whatever she saw must be bad.

"There's a barrier. No way we can escape that way."

They couldn't lead the hounds to all those people. It would be a slaughter.

"What do We do?"

"I don't knoW." Maria sounded on the verge of tears.

Conryu kneW. He just hoped Maria didn't hate him, assuming he somehoW survived.

He Worked his hand free of her grip and lunged left betWeen a pair of stalls. If he could draW the hounds aWay she'd have a chance of escaping

"Conryu!" Maria screamed after him

He ignored her pained shout Conryu needed an open space, someWhere they couldn't sneak up on him He had to keep the things busy long enough for everyone to escape

Straight ahead Was the petting zoo. The panicked animals had smashed the fence and fled, leaving a round opening. He doubted he'd find anything better.

A chill on his back Was the only Warning he got. Conryu leapt to the right, rolled, and sprang back to his feet.

The tWo shadoW hounds stood facing him, Wisps of darkness rising off them like steam, jagged black fangs filling their mouths

They circled right and Conryu Went left, trying to keep the monsters in front of him. He Wished he kneW more about them. Unlike Maria, this Was all neW to him.

The hounds rushed him

One leapt high for his throat and the other lunged loW for his legs. Conryu jumped and tWisted, going over one and under the other. Passing so close betWeen them left him shaking With cold

All at once it greW brighter. The hounds Whined and some of the Warmth returned to Conryu's shaking body.

The whines turned to snarls as the hounds gathered themselves to leap again

Lances of white light shot out, piercing their sides and driving the monsters to the ground More beams, these orange as flames, came from another direction, engulfing the hounds and burning them to nothing

"Conryu!" Mrs. Kane waved at him, her hands still crackling with white light.

Conryu slumped to his knees. It was over, for now anyway. He'd survived, though he doubted his mother would ever let him out of the apartment again

* * *

Maria hit him with a flying tackle, wrapping her arms around his neck and crying at the same time. "You scared me to death! I ought to slug you for ditching me like that. What were you thinking?"

"Let him breathe, dear " Mrs Kane placed her hand on his back and warmth and energy flowed into him.

Conryu had never been healed by a wizard before, but if it felt like this he wouldn't mind doing it again. Maria shifted, settling onto his lap. "Thanks, Mrs. Kane. If you hadn't gotten here when you did I'm not sure I could have dodged those things again "

"It's a wonder you dodged them once," another voice said.

Conryu moved Maria a bit to the side so he could see who was speaking. It was the blond wizard from the Department, Terra. She must have shot the fire blast.

"Thanks for the help. Where'd those things come from?"

"That's what we're here to determine," Terra said.

"We?" Maria looked at her mother.

Mrs. Kane nodded. "Your father asked me to lend a hand. Since it's a Weekend I didn't have any client meetings so I agreed. We Would have been here sooner, but We didn't expect the barrier"

Maria froWned. "HoW did you knoW We needed your help in the first place?"

"Conryu's ring. It does more than provide protection. I can also monitor his surroundings through it. I sensed the dark energy the moment you entered the grounds. We rushed here as fast as We could."

"Shizuku," Terra said.

The tone in her voice grabbed Conryu's attention. He craned his neck and looked around Maria's head. Three bodies Were shambling toWard them in bloodstained clothes. Their eyes Were nothing but black pits and faint, echoing moans filled the air around them He and Maria scrambled to their feet

"First shadoW hounds and noW zombies." Mrs. Kane raised her hands and chanted a spell. A stream of fire shot out toWard the undead. The fire struck a barrier of darkness and sputtered to nothing

The zombies kept coming.

The Department Wizard cast a fire spell of her oWn, stronger than the one Maria's mother used judging by the amount of heat coming off it. After just a second a sheen of sWeat covered Conryu's chest.

Despite the extra heat the zombies kept coming. The Department Wizard jogged over to them and the group backed aWay, putting more space betWeen them and the undead.

"Magic's not going to do it, Terra," Mrs. Kane said. "Their darkness aura's too strong."

"We could bury them with earth magic," Terra said.

"They'd just dig themselves out. We need to force our magic through their barrier "

"Force it through how?" Maria asked.

"Direct physical contact " Terra ground her teeth as the zombies continued to advance.

"I can do it," Conryu said.

"That's crazy." Maria grabbed his arm. "You'll get yourself killed."

"She's right." Mrs. Kane shook her head. "I can't let you take that kind of a risk."

"What risk? Those things are so slow I could run circles around them. They're getting closer and we're running out of time "

"He's got a point, Shizuku," Terra said. "One spell per fist ought to do it "

"There are three of them," Maria said

"Put one on my right foot." Conryu clenched his fists and held them out

The two wizards exchanged looks, raised their hands, and began to cast

"Mom, no!"

Mrs. Kane ignored Maria and kept chanting. It felt like his hands were in an open oven, hot, but not painful. Terra finished first and began again, this time pointing her hands at his right foot

When both wizards had finished their spells Terra said, "Make solid contact to the head or chest. The spell will detonate with a one-second delay so in and out fast. Got it?"

"No sWeat."

Conryu rushed the leftmost zombie. It had on greasy overalls and tools dangled half in and half out of its pockets. It moaned louder and shambled toWard Conryu.

He darted in, punched it right betWeen the eyes, and leapt back. The zombie exploded into flames. The others ignored their burning comrade and shuffled toWard him.

Conryu leapt betWeen them, punching one in the head and kicking the second in the chest as he fleW by. They both burst into flames.

He rolled to his feet and spun, ready for another round He needn't have bothered. The first zombie Was nothing but ash and the others Weren't far behind.

Maria ran over and hugged him. Jonny and Rin had caught up at some point and they joined the group.

"We need some marshmalloWs," Jonny said.

"Or chestnuts," Rin added.

"Chestnuts roasting on an open zombie." Conryu grinned. "Got a nice ring to it "

"Are you all crazy?" Maria looked up at him. "You could have been killed. TWice."

"But I Wasn't. So What noW?"

"NoW you kids go home and let us handle the rest," Terra said. Sirens Wailed in the distance. "The cavalry Will arrive soon. If there are any more zombies the police can shoot them for us."

* * *

Conryu Worked himself free of Maria after a minute or tWo. It Wasn't that he didn't like having her Wrapped around him, but it made it hard to breathe When she squeezed him so tight. Out near the fence the police had set up a cordon and were getting the people out in a semi-orderly fashion. There really didn't seem to be much for them to do at the moment

"We need to find the source of that spell," Terra said.

Mrs. Kane turned to him and Maria. "I trust you two can make your way back to the apartment on your own? I've strengthened the wards so you'll have nothing to fear there."

"Sure, Mom, no problem," Maria said

"We have a great deal to discuss," Mrs. Kane said. "Perhaps we should all have dinner together tonight. I'm sure your parents would appreciate an explanation, Conryu."

"I expect they would, and they aren't the only ones."

Mrs. Kane nodded. "Our apartment then, as long as Sho and Connie don't mind."

"I'll tell them. Thanks again." Conryu led Maria off toward the parking lot with Jonny and Rin tagging along behind. "Think we can get out of here before the press arrives?"

"I don't think so." Maria pointed at a pair of satellite dishes rising in the distance

"Damn them all! Am I going to have to dodge those vultures for the rest of my life?"

"Nope. No press allowed at the academy. Only teachers and students"

Conryu grinned. "Finally something to look forward to. How did you know what those things were? Your mom teach you?"

"About the shadow hounds, yes. A lot of what I know comes from The Basics of Wizardry. All the girls have to take it junior year. It's a national requirement. Thanks to you, I bet the boys have to take it starting next year."

"They're not going to let you come back to the carnival next year, dude," Jonny said.

Conryu barked a humorless laugh. "I ought to sue. I've heard about the danger of carnival rides, but this is ridiculous."

When the little group reached the exit a mob of reporters had gathered behind a line of yellow tape. A dozen cops attempted to keep them under control. Detective Chang Was talking With the Woman in the cloWn outfit and jotting doWn notes. He noticed Conryu, ended his intervieW, and headed their Way.

"You okay, Conryu?"

"Sure. No ongoing threat, huh?"

Detective Chang looked aWay then back. "What I should have said Was, no ongoing threat from the True Face of God cult. This Was clearly something else."

"HoW can you be sure?" Conryu asked.

"Because they used magic," Maria answered for the detective. "The cultists hate all magic and Would never have anything to do With it."

"What she said. I'm still investigating the guy from yesterday. Since you Were attacked again I got the call in case it Was related."

"Is it related?" Conryu asked.

"Way too soon to say, but if I Was you I'd lie loW. You guys Want an escort home?"

Conryu shook his head. Regular cops Wouldn't be much use against magical attacks. "I'll take an escort through the reporters."

"No problem." Detective Chang Whistled to draW his men's attention. "Let's make these kids a path."

Six officers made a circle around Conryu and his friends then proceeded to push their way through the gathered throng All manner of questions were shouted, most of which he didn't know the answer to and wouldn't have answered if he did

When they reached the edge of the throng the officers made a gap for Conryu and the others then shifted to block the reporters from following

"Later, bro " Jonny broke off to head for his bike, a piece of crap import that Conryu had helped him fix up

"I'll be going too " Rin hugged Maria and trotted off to her little car

"Just you and me," Conryu said

Maria took his hand and the pair continued on to where he'd parked his bike They arrived to find Kat Gabel dressed pretty as you please in black slacks and a crisp white blouse leaning on his handlebars Conryu frowned, both because she was there in the first place and had the nerve to touch his bike without permission

"You can't take a hint, can you?" Conryu asked

Kat shrugged "I wouldn't be much good at my job if I took no for an answer What happened in there?"

"How should I know?" He grabbed Maria's helmet and handed it to her When he reached for his the reporter snatched it first and held it above her head "Are you kidding me?"

She danced away "Answer my questions and I'll give it back "

A deep spring of anger welled up in Conryu After everything that had happened over the last three days he didn't have the patience to deal with this It was a game to her, nothing but another story. She didn't care what happened to him, she just wanted a scoop.

He darted forward, leapt, and kicked the helmet out of her hands and straight up into the air. When he landed Conryu immediately gathered himself and jumped again, snatching the helmet out of the air. He turned a flip and landed behind her.

The reporter stared at him, mouth hanging partway open.

"Here's all I have to say. If you'd pass it along to your colleagues I'd appreciate it. No. Fucking. Comment."

He jammed the helmet over his head and climbed on in front of Maria. They thundered out of the parking lot, leaving the still-staring reporter in a cloud of dust

Chapter 4

Investigation

Shizuku watched Maria and Conryu make their way toward the exit of the carnival grounds It was an absolute miracle the shadow hounds hadn't killed anyone, especially Conryu Even if the beasts hadn't intended it, a single brush with fang or claw could have seriously injured or even killed someone in the crowd

And then zombies Who ever heard of zombies with a dark aura that negated powerful fire magic? If Conryu hadn't been able to deliver the magic physically they might have been in trouble He certainly had his father's skill when it came to fighting It would be interesting to see what he could accomplish in the realm of magic

She brushed loose grass off her knees while Terra watched with an impatient frown Terra hadn't been thrilled about getting called in on a Sunday, but with a blatant attack on a public venue Orin hadn't had any choice The police only had one wizard on their staff, a not especially powerful wind mage This sort of investigation was definitely a job for the Department

Shizuku didn't mind lending a hand considering it was her family—and she certainly considered Conryu a member of her family—being targeted. That she had to work with Terra and not Clair was a relief. Clair had been in her grade at the academy and they'd never gotten along.

Shizuku chanted in the divine tongue, "Reveal the hidden darkness." The spell should reveal the source of the hounds as well as the dark aura that surrounded the zombies. She repeated the words over and over, gently directing the white mist that served as the spell's visible manifestation around the area. Soon an inky, insubstantial line appeared.

A wave of her hand sent the mist rushing along in the same direction as the line, following it to its source. Terra fell in behind her as they traced the spell through the grounds. All the visitors had left so they had no trouble making their way to the center of the park.

A gray, stone construct filled an area several hundred yards in diameter. It resembled a small mountain, with a shadowed cave entrance straight ahead. The line went right inside, getting thicker as they drew closer to the source. Beside her Terra muttered a spell of her own, this one in the language of earth. A little quaver ran through the ground in response to the magic.

"It was raised by mundane means," Terra said. "The exterior only looks like stone, it's actually some sort of light-weight composite."

Shizuku nodded. It was hardly likely that the carnival kept a wizard capable of raising such a structure on their payroll.

Terra conjured a ball of flame in her right hand, pushing back the gloom. "Let's head in."

"Whoa, hold on there " A skinny man with a pockmarked face, bald head, and filthy clothes came running toward them waving his hands "You can't take open flames into the Haunted Cavern "

"Who are you and why can't we?" Terra asked in her official voice, the one that made people who didn't work for the government cringe

"For one thing, most of the props inside are flammable, not to mention the hydraulic fluid that runs them and the cart You go in there carrying that ball of fire and whoosh, I'm out three hundred grand and one star attraction and you'll be needing to regrow your hair "

"Is that what happened to you?" Terra asked

He rubbed his bald pate "Naw, mine just fell out There are some flashlights inside you ladies can use Would that work for you?"

Terra spoke a single, harsh syllable and the flame in her hand vanished "It will, especially since you'll be joining us to hold one of them "

"I will?"

"Yes, you will You seem a knowledgeable fellow and we may have questions Just who are you anyway?"

"Beg your pardon, miss Wilbur Cullen at your service I own this carnival It's been in the Cullen family for over a hundred years We crisscross the country every year following the island an—"

"That's fascinating, Mr Cullen, but we really need to move this investigation along so if you'd direct us to those flashlights, that would be great " Terra motioned him toward the ride

Shizuku watched the interaction with silent amusement. She couldn't speak without ruining her detection spell, but Terra said enough for both of them. Terra herded Wilbur toward the ride like a collie chasing a sheep. Shizuku trusted Terra to keep a look out for any threats while she focused on the line that led ever deeper into the artificial caverns.

Ten feet inside the entrance a track started. Three cars that bore a vague resemblance to mine carts waited for passengers that wouldn't be arriving that day. Wilbur went to a utility cabinet hanging to one side of the tracks and removed a pair of long flashlights. Terra accepted one and clicked it on.

The flashlight's beam did little to dispel the cavern's gloom. The still-functioning darkness spell must be suppressing the light. Shizuku didn't know why the spell was still active since it had already summoned the shadow hounds and animated the zombies, but it was clearly doing something.

"Which way?" Terra asked.

Shizuku motioned straight ahead. They followed the tracks deeper into the cavern. Plastic demons hung limp from the hydraulic pistons that made them jump out to scare the passengers. The ride looked quite realistic. Whoever had designed the artificial stone had done a good job. No wonder this was a popular ride

"This is our last carnival until the island returns next year," Wilbur said. "Do you think we'll be able to open back up?"

"I wouldn't count on it," Terra said. "This is the site of an active investigation. Besides, after what happened this morning I doubt you'd find many people willing to return."

"Suppose you're right We had a good Saturday at least Everyone wanted to go through the Haunted Cavern Food sales were good too We should at least break even on this stop"

"I'm thrilled for you," Terra said "Please stop talking now"

"Sorry I talk when I'm nervous"

The black line turned off the main tracks a little ways ahead, where there was a shadowed recess in the wall Shizuku stopped, grabbed Terra's robe, and pointed at the spot where it disappeared

"Through there?" Terra turned to Wilbur "What's in there?"

"It's a maintenance access so we can service the machinery and disassemble the ride"

Both flashlights swung in, illuminating the interior of the maintenance space In the largest open area a corpse wearing a polka dot dress floated above a spell circle inscribed with dark energy that sparked with red light

Shizuku released her spell "Now I see why the spell is still operating The corpse is maintaining a necromantic loop"

"Aw, Gerty" Wilbur moaned softly

"Do you know her?" Terra asked with surprising gentleness

"Gerty's our bookkeeper I hadn't seen her all day today Thought she was sick Her stomach never has worked just right"

"Did she have family?" Shizuku asked

"We were all her family, but no kids or husband if that's what you mean She was devoted to the carnival Gerty worked here since she was fourteen" Wilbur sniffed and wiped his eyes

"Perhaps you'd like to Wait outside?" Terra said. "It Won't take us long to deal With this. I'm afraid the police Will Want to examine your friend's body."

"I understand. And I think I Will take you up on your offer and Wait outside. Be gentle. Gerty Was a good girl." Wilbur fled the maintenance room

When Wilbur had made himself scarce the tWo Wizards shared a look. "This isn't going to be easy," Shizuku said. "The dark magic has latched on to the body. Whoever set this trap did a poor job of it."

"It's an ugly casting, no doubt, but it did What the Wizard Wanted it to so you can't call it a complete failure. Whoever is responsible probably didn't care What happened after the hounds Were summoned and the zombies raised."

"Maybe not." Shizuku pursed her lips. "But if We don't break the spell and dissipate the necromantic energy properly the body Will explode and release a lethal miasma over a square mile at least. It could kill thousands."

"Well, We'll just have to do the job right. HoW do you Want to handle it?" Terra asked.

"I'm Weakest in dark magic so you should disable the spell circle. I'll craft a siphon of Wind and light to disperse the gathered energy Well above the city. Worst case We end up With a feW dead birds and acid rain "

"Given the alternative, I can live With that. HoW long do you need to construct the siphon?"

"Fifteen minutes "

"Let's begin."

Shizuku tried to block out the guttural demonic language Terra used to unravel the spell circle. While she got excellent grades at the academy, Shizuku had never managed even the most basic of dark spells. She simply couldn't get the magic to work for her. It was like her body rejected the Infernal power out of hand

She began her casting by crafting a framework of light magic running from just above the circle, down the tunnel and out into the sky. That was the easy part. Next she switched to wind magic and conjured what amounted to a contained tornado inside the framework. Finally she bound the two spells together to make a stronger, cohesive whole. Not the most complex spell she'd ever created, but challenging enough given the circumstances

A chill ran through her and she turned her attention to Terra. The circle had partly broken and wisps of dark energy oozed out of the body's eyes and mouth. The crimson flecks were promptly sucked up into Shizuku's funnel. Everything seemed to be working the way it should. So why was she so worried?

* * *

"Oh, shit!" After twenty minutes of listening to Terra chant in Infernal the human words jarred Shizuku.

It took only a second to figure out what prompted them. Dark energy swirled around the body in red waves, pressing into it instead of getting sucked up into her funnel. It didn't look like an explosion was imminent, but something had clearly gone wrong.

"What happened?"

"I used a conjecture where I should have used a constant. The spell's broken and spiraling out of control."

"Out of control how?" Shizuku asked.

"Best case it Will exhaust itself, destroying the body in the process"

"And the Worst case?"

"It'll continue to build, eventually exploding and taking the entire park With it."

"Shit"

"Yeah"

Shizuku ran a hand through her hair. "HoW do We stop it?"

"There's no stopping it noW. All We can do is contain it, or try to anyWay."

"Okay, I can do a light barrier if you handle earth. Then I'll adjust my funnel to draW anything that escapes up and aWay from the city"

They hadn't even begun to cast When the body moved. It turned its head toWard them, eyes burning With Infernal light. The gloW from the circle vanished as all the poWer rushed into the corpse. The body fell to the ground Where it began to rise. A dark aura surrounded it, similar, but different from the zombies. She didn't think this aura Would stop their spells, but that begged the question of What it did do.

The creature's teeth and nails lengthened. Green ichor dripped from them, sizzling Where it struck the floor. It snarled at them and took a step.

Shizuku chanted, "Divine chains hold all things in place, Heaven's Binding!"

Chains of White light appeared around the reanimated body. It fought, struggling to break free. Dark energy sent cracks running all through the binding

That answered one question. It was an aura of decay. If it got close to them the magic would rot flesh as easily as the magical bindings

A chain shattered. At this rate it would escape in moments. She spoke a reinforcing spell, but that wouldn't last long either. The aura of darkness broke down her magic as quickly as she strengthened it

Pain throbbed at her temples as Shizuku struggled to maintain the binding and the funnel They needed to end this before the monster escaped. Unlike the shadow hounds, this one wouldn't simply hunt down Conryu, it would kill anyone it encountered. It had gone completely out of control and feral.

"Terra, burn it "

"What about the dark energy?"

"My funnel's still in place." Shizuku grimaced against a fresh spasm of pain. "But I can't hold this thing for long."

Terra chanted in the language of fire, thrust her hands out, and sent a river of flame roaring into the undead monster. Another quick incantation contained the flame so it didn't spread to any of the flammables in the maintenance room.

The magical flames ate away at the undead's protective aura even as the aura rotted Shizuku's binding. The combined magics were wearing it down, but too slowly.

Another chain broke and still the undead fought even as the flames consumed it little by little. Not much remained of Gerty's body, just a charred skeleton, but it struggled with all its might to escape Shizuku's spell.

A third chain shattered, leaving only two. The backlash sent a sharp pain stabbing into her eye

The light magic binding wouldn't hold. Though she wasn't as strong in earth magic, Shizuku chanted, "Fists of stone, bind and hold, Stone Grasp!" Stone blocks thrust up from the ground and bound the undead's feet in place.

Shizuku's stomach churned and she nearly vomited.

Just a little longer.

Mustering every scrap of her rapidly diminishing strength Shizuku chanted an augmenting fire spell and Terra's flames turned from orange to blue Thirty seconds later the undead skeleton collapsed and the ashes swirled up the funnel and out of the artificial mountain.

Shizuku released all her spells and fell to her knees, utterly spent, head throbbing with the mother of all migraines. Terra rushed over beside her. "You hurt?"

"Tired. Maintaining four spells is about my limit. I think we underestimated our opponent. That spell wasn't running out of control, it just appeared to be. Whoever set it up used the residual energy to create that undead creature, forcing us to destroy the body before we could examine it."

"If you're right, and I'm inclined to think you are, then we're dealing with an extremely talented wizard." Terra grasped Shizuku's hand and pulled her to her feet.

"Worse," Shizuku said. "A necromancer. Only someone specialized in creating undead could have managed a casting that powerful and subtle."

Shizuku really didn't want to cast another spell right then, but she had to know for sure. "Reveal."

The simple detection spell showed all the dark energy had dissipated. She sighed and relaxed a fraction. They were safe for the moment

* * *

Lin's stomach finally settled when Conryu's bike roared out of the parking lot He knew it wasn't the young man's fault that horrible things kept happening in his vicinity, but that didn't change the fact that everyone would be much safer with Conryu elsewhere As a bonus, most of the reporters appeared to have lost interest now that the main attraction had gone home

He walked back to the shack where he'd left the welcome clown She sat on a folding chair, her white face paint smeared from crying Since the woman hadn't even seen whatever had caused the panic Lin assumed the loss of today's gate had brought on the tears

Lin flipped open his notebook "So you were saying everything seemed normal today You didn't see anyone odd in the area, a strange woman maybe?"

She sniffed "Why would you assume it was a woman?"

"Because whoever did this had to be a wizard Think hard "

The clown shook her head "Sorry, I just don't remember anything out of the ordinary "

Lin nodded He wasn't going to get anything useful out of her He dug a card with his number as well as the station's on it "If you should think of anything, please contact us right away "

She accepted the card and Lin turned to leave His eyes went wide A black cloud rose from the center of the carnival That couldn't be natural

He tucked his notepad away and ran towards the source He couldn't do much about magic, but he needed to make sure no civilians remained in the area

The only person anyWhere near the artificial mountain Was a bald, middle-aged man sitting on a picnic table rubbing his hands together and staring at the tunnel's opening. He didn't seem aWare of Lin's approach.

"Sir." The bald guy finally looked his Way. "You should move aWay. It's not safe."

He laughed, but it sounded more bitter than amused "You're telling me. My bookkeeper's body is in there floating over some gloWing circle and noW there's literally a dark cloud hanging over my business. I'm not sure What else could go Wrong."

"Are you the oWner of this carnival?"

He nodded. "Wilbur Cullen. And you are?"

Lin shoWed Wilbur his badge. "Do you mind if I ask you some questions, preferably a safe distance from here?"

"Ask aWay, sonny, but I'm not going anyWhere until those Wizards come out and tell me What in the World is going on With my carnival "

Lin shook his head in despair. "Did you see anything unusual today?"

"No, everything Was the same as every other day. Line formed early, figured We'd have a good take. ShoWs What thinking gets you. It'll be a miracle if the city lets us come back next year."

"If it's any consolation, Mr. Cullen, since no one Was hurt and the incident Wasn't your fault I'm confident the city council Will let you return next year. That's What I'll say if anyone asks."

Wilbur seemed to see him for the first time. "Thank you for that. I hope you find Whoever did this, but there's nothing I can tell you "

"Who's in charge of maintaining the ride? Perhaps they saw something out of the ordinary."

"That'd be the Carrigton boys. Not much brains, but damn good mechanics"

"Where can I find them?"

"Hell if I know. Those things showed up and everybody scattered all over creation. When the ladies finish up I'll run you back to the boys' trailer. If they aren't there I don't know what to tell you"

Lin tried to think of another way to come at this, but nothing occurred to him. Maybe the wizards would have something useful to tell him

A rumble and roar came from the ride followed by a dull red glow that filled the mouth of the cave. It looked like the mouth of Hell

"That's a damn good trick," Wilbur muttered. "We could probably duplicate that effect with tinted lights, make the ride look even more ominous."

Apparently Wilbur wasn't so shook up he couldn't still think about business. The glow vanished and the cloud overhead dissipated. Lin let out a breath. It looked like the threat had ended

As if to prove it the wizards emerged from the ride. The shorter one, a woman of Imperial descent wearing a black suit, looked like every step pained her. Wilbur marched over and Lin joined him.

"Where's Gerty?"

The taller one in gray, a Department wizard for sure, shook her head. "There was a secondary spell that destroyed the body so We couldn't examine it. I'm sorry, but there's nothing left but ash."

Wilbur Wandered aWay staring at the sky and shaking his head.

"And Who might you be?" the tall Wizard asked.

Lin flashed his badge. "I'm investigating the attempted murder of Conryu Koda. Since he Was involved in this incident as Well I got the call. Do you think they're related, miss?"

"Just Terra, please. Since the Department assigned me to head the investigation of the magical aspect of the assault, I figure We'll be seeing more of each other."

"You read my mind. Perhaps We can share information and Work the case together."

Terra nodded "Good idea."

The other Wizard groaned. "I'm heading home. I need a nap before I talk to Conryu's parents."

"Okay, Shizuku. Will you bring the chief up to date?"

Shizuku nodded and trudged off.

"Will she be okay?" Lin asked.

"Shizuku's stronger than she looks. A feW hours' sleep and a good meal Will set her back to form. She channeled a lot of poWer dealing With the undead inside."

"Undead?" Lin tried to Wrap his mind around that announcement and failed. He'd studied a variety of magical threats in the police academy, but the instructors alWays said to let the Department Wizard handle them. This case Was looking more and more beyond his capabilities

"Yeah." Terra headed over to a pair of picnic tables. "Let's sit and talk. I think We have a good deal to discuss."

* * *

Conryu swung his bike into the parking garage and down to his space He'd been tense the whole ride home and now his back and shoulders were killing him At least nothing had tried to kill them on the road He almost laughed What was the world coming to when making a fifteen-minute drive without something trying to kill you seemed like a major victory?

Apparently even crazy wizards and lunatic cultists had their limits Thank goodness for that To top it off he'd forgotten to pick up his mother's caramel corn

He and Maria swung down off the bike and hung their helmets on the handlebars Maria grinned "I thought that reporter was going to have a heart attack when you kicked the helmet out of her hands "

"I probably shouldn't have done that, but I couldn't help it I was so sick of those people and their questions My life is none of their damn business Do you suppose she took the hint?"

"For a day or two maybe " Maria took his hand and they walked to the elevator "You should go straight home Your parents are probably worried sick "

"I don't know " Conryu hit the button for his floor "Mom doesn't usually watch the news on Sunday and since my phone isn't ringing I bet she doesn't even know what happened "

The door slid shut and they started up When they'd gone three floors Maria hit the emergency stop

"Wha—"

She kissed him, a long, deep kiss that left him struggling to breathe Her hand slipped up under his shirt and ran over his chest

He grabbed her wrists and gently pushed her away. "What are you doing?"

"What do you think?" She pressed closer.

Conryu took a step back, but he hit the elevator wall. There was nowhere to run and part of him didn't want to. Another part, the rational part, didn't want to screw things up with the best friend he'd ever had.

"I thought we talked about this last year. We said it was better to stay just friends. That anything more would be too awkward."

"We did." She lunged at him, forcing Conryu to spin around her and slip to the other side of the elevator.

There wasn't much room to maneuver in a six-by-six box. She turned to face him once more, a hungry gleam in her eyes. "We were almost killed today. It was clarifying. I don't want to die without being with you at least once. This is a no-strings-attached thing. If you want to pretend nothing happened after it's fine with me."

When Maria came at him again he didn't dodge. Conryu caught her in a tight embrace. "It's not okay with me. I love you. Whether as a best friend or girlfriend or both I'm not sure. But I know this: a quickie in an elevator is not how we're going to end one phase and begin another. And we're not going to let the stress of the moment ruin a lifelong relationship."

Maria was shaking in his arms and a moment later tears soaked his shirt. He held her for a while, not saying anything.

She looked up at him and he smiled. "You okay?"

"I was so scared those shadow hounds were going to kill you. Then the zombies. Then when you were safe I felt so relieved

I was afraid I might pass out. I guess the emotions got the best of me. I'm sorry."

"Don't be." Conryu brushed the hair out of her eyes. "When warriors survive a battle the aftermath leaves them horny as hell. I read in one of Dad's books that it was because in ancient times so many died in battle those who survived had an overwhelming need to rebuild the population. Personally I think it's a mix of adrenalin and other hormones mingling and messing with your brain."

They moved apart and he flipped the switch to start the elevator moving again Maria smoothed his shirt, her hand lingering a moment on his chest sending a thrill through him He took her hand and held it. He was only human after all and if she kept that up...

"What are you going to tell your mom?" Maria asked.

"About this? Not a thing."

"You know what I mean."

He shrugged. "The truth. Though I think I'll leave the details to your mom. I don't really understand exactly what happened anyway."

The bell rang and the door slid open on Conryu's floor. "You want to come in and hang out for a while?"

"No, I need a little time to collect myself and take a cold shower. I'll see you at dinner."

Conryu stepped out and the door slid shut, sending Maria up to the penthouse. He gave a little shake of his head and made the short walk to his apartment. What a day. It was only a little after noon and he was completely wiped out. Maybe he could take a nap, and a cold shower didn't sound bad either.

He opened the door and found his mother sitting on the couch staring at the tv. Behind a hot, blond reporter Was the carnival With the headline "Chaos at the Carnival!" A moment later Conryu's face came on screen.

"Hi, Mom "

She spun "You are never leaving the building again "

* * *

Lin and Terra sat across from each other, each sizing the other up. They'd exchanged information and Were digesting What the other had said. Lin had Worked With the police Wizard once before, but only briefly. He Wasn't certain about the protocol. Would she take the lead or Would they each handle their oWn aspects of the investigation alone and compare notes occasionally?

He took a drink, trying to gather his thoughts. Wilbur had been kind enough to provide them With bottles of Water at cost. The idea of not making a profit galled the man, but given everything that had happened he seemed to think he oWed them.

"So What do you make of all this?" Lin asked.

"Beyond the fact that someone Wants Conryu dead very badly, I'm not sure of anything. We can't even confirm that the cultist and the necromancer are connected, though it seems beyond comprehension that they aren't."

"Agreed. The cultist, Mr. Call, had contact With someone on an encrypted forum the night before the attack. I'll Wager Whoever that Was is our link. What I'm curious about is, hoW did the Wizard knoW Conryu Would be here today? After the first attack there's no reason to think he'd even leave home."

Terra shook her head, sending her thick, grayish-blond hair flying. "I wondered about that myself. That trap was set a while ago, late last night or early this morning I'd guess. I'm not even certain whoever set it intended the trap for him. It's entirely possible whoever's responsible simply adapted whatever was already here to kill Conryu."

Lin's jaw clenched and he forced himself to relax. This was how it always went at the start of an investigation. He needed to be patient and do the job. "We need more facts and less guesswork. What do you say we go talk to the Carrigton brothers?"

"Excellent suggestion, Detective. We could sit here and bandy ideas back and forth until nightfall, but that's not going to get us anywhere."

Lin stood and waved to draw Wilbur's attention. The carnival owner had been pacing and muttering ever since he'd learned the body of his friend was destroyed. Lin didn't blame him. Finding out the body of someone you'd known for fifteen years had been used in a dark magic ritual would bother anyone.

Wilbur hustled over. His eyes were red from crying, though he appeared under control for the moment. "You two want to go meet the Carrigton boys?"

"Exactly right," Lin said.

They followed Wilbur toward the far end of the carnival, past empty game booths and silent rides, out to what resembled a trailer park. Tractor trailers were parked beside campers with dozens of rusty pickups mixed in for good measure.

Wilbur led them to a small camper, maybe fifteen feet long, still hooked behind a pickup that Lin suspected was older than him. The only discernible color in it Was rust. The carnival oWner Walked up to the slightly askeW front door and knocked.

There Was no reply or sound from inside. Lin reached for his gun, a tWisty feeling in the pit of his stomach.

"Hey!" Wilbur shouted. "Wake up, you tWo. The police Want to talk to you."

Still nothing

"Mr Cullen " Lin had his pistol out and ready "Please step aWay from the door, sir."

Wilbur stared at Lin's gun, his eyes bugging out. "No need for that. Those idiots probably got drunk and passed out on their couch "

"Mr Cullen, please "

Wilbur moved aside, shaking his head. When Wilbur had gone fifty feet and taken cover behind a heavy-duty haul trailer, Lin reached for the camper door. Of course it Was locked.

"Let me." Terra placed her finger on the lock and spoke some Words in What Lin assumed Was one of the magical languages. The lock popped open and she moved aside. "After you "

Lin tugged the door open and Went up the tWo iron steps into the camper. The place Was empty unless you counted garbage. It only took a minute to clear the tiny trailer. There Was nothing much to see beyond a mountain of empty beer cans, several equally empty Whiskey bottles, and Wrappers from the concession stands. The Carrigton brothers clearly didn't live the healthiest lifestyle

"It's clear."

Terra hopped up the steps and grimaced. "This day just keeps getting Worse. No sign of the brothers?"

"No Once we have a look around I'll have to get a description from Mr Cullen I need to call the crime scene guys out here too I doubt they'll find anything, but it couldn't hurt to have them check " Lin dug a pair of rubber gloves out of his pocket and handed them to Terra They looked huge on her tiny hands, but at least she wouldn't leave prints everywhere

Lin called for the crime scene unit while Terra looked around They would be there in twenty minutes, which gave them a little time to try and figure out what happened

"Did you find anything?" Lin asked

"No Who lives like this?" She held up a dirty plate with what appeared to be dried cheese on it

Lin shrugged He'd seen worse in a flophouse downtown "The techs will have a better chance of finding something than us "

Lin left the camper Wilbur was peeking around the corner of the trailer so Lin waved him over Wilbur rushed to join him "Are they okay?"

"I don't know, but the trailer's empty What did the missing men look like?"

"Oh god, not the boys too Are we cursed, Detective? My people haven't hurt anyone We just try to make a living the best way we know how "

"There's no curse " Terra came down out of the camper "I'd sense it if there were What you have is a serious case of bad luck Someone has decided to use your carnival for their own evil purposes "

"I'm not certain that's better," Wilbur said

"The description, sir?" Lin asked

Wilbur slipped a bottle out of his pocket and took a long pull. "They're twins, dark hair and eyes, usually in greasy overalls."

Terra gasped. "You said they worked on the ride where we found your friend?"

"That's right, why?"

"I guess there's no easy way to say this. Their bodies were raised as zombies by the same spell that summoned the hounds. We were forced to destroy them as well. I'm very sorry."

Wilbur wavered and Lin grabbed him before he fell. "We're cursed." He spoke so softly Lin almost didn't hear him.

"Will you be okay, sir?" When Wilbur nodded Lin sent the carnival owner on his way.

"How is he?" Terra asked.

Lin shook his head. "How do you think? What in the world have we gotten into?"

* * *

Conryu hadn't been able to sleep, but the shower and clean clothes had done him a world of good. He sprawled on the couch half watching some stupid cartoon. Maria had called an hour ago and said dinner was at seven. Dad sat at the kitchen table reading, content with washing his face and putting on a fresh shirt. Mom, on the other hand, had been fussing in the mirror since he hung up with Maria. You'd think it was dinner at the mayor's mansion instead of a casual meal with people they'd known their whole lives

It was now five of seven and if they didn't step on it they'd be late. At long last Mom bustled out of the bedroom in a blue dress and pearls, her hair done up with some sort of clamps that looked like they could be used to extract a confession.

"Are you sure Shizuku wants us to come? We could have hosted them here "

"Mom, relax Mrs Kane definitely invited us up There's probably some magic book or other she wants to show us after we eat " Conryu clicked the tv off "We ready?"

Mom grabbed her purse and the three of them made the short walk to the elevator When they reached the elaborate penthouse door Conryu knocked Maria opened it a moment later The scent of meat and spices wafted out, distracting him from the red kimono she was wearing

"Come on in " Maria stepped aside and motioned them through

Conryu went first, pausing to kick his boots off in the little depression just inside the door Five paces beyond the entryway the apartment opened up into a dining room with a cherry table long enough to seat twenty Six places had been set with pale plates and a selection of knives and forks A bottle of red wine sat near the head of the table A crystal chandelier lit the space and gave it an extra air of opulence

"Is that Giovanni's lasagna I smell?" Conryu asked, his mouth already watering

Maria grinned and led them into the dining room "Sure is Mom didn't feel like cooking so we ordered takeout I assured her you wouldn't object "

"Good call "

Mr Kane emerged from a side door, a bright if somewhat forced smile on his face It was rare to find him in jeans and t-shirt instead of his usual suit "Conryu, I trust you're recovered from your adventure this morning Connie, you're looking lovely tonight "

Mom scowled at him, prompting a hurried turn to Dad. "Sho, always nice to see you."

Dad nodded and they shook hands. "Everything under control, Orin? You're looking a little rough around the edges."

"Yes," Mom said. "What's being done to make sure my son will be kept safe?"

Mr. Kane winced. "I have my best wizard investigating. Rest assured she'll get to the bottom of it. In the meantime, everyone please sit. Shizuku is putting the finishing touches on dinner and by that I mean transferring it from the delivery containers to nice plates. She'll be along in a moment. Can I offer anyone a drink?"

Mom took him up on the offer instantly and downed her first glass in three big gulps. Mr. Kane refilled her glass without comment.

A couple minutes of forced chitchat came to a merciful end when Mrs. Kane emerged from the kitchen with plates full of Italian delicacies drifting behind her. Conryu had trouble deciding whether to focus on Mrs. Kane in her blue-and-gold silk kimono or the food. It was easy to see where Maria got her looks. The food settled on the table.

"Everyone, dig in," Mrs. Kane said. "And no business talk until we finish the cookies."

Twenty minutes and three helpings later Conryu licked the last of the sauce off his lips, savoring the tangy flavor. "That was awesome, Mrs. Kane. I'd fight shadow hounds every day if it ended with a spread like this."

Mom almost choked on her wine. "That wasn't funny, Conryu."

He'd only been partially joking, but decided not to point that out. "Seriously, it was great."

"Thank you, dear." Mrs. Kane gestured and spoke a short phrase in a language he didn't recognize. The dirty plates floated off, leaving the table clean. "I suppose we'd best get down to business."

Mrs. Kane filled them in on everything they'd discovered at the carnival and Mr. Kane chimed in with what Terra and Detective Lin had come up with so far. When they finished Mom was staring in horror and Dad's eyebrows had drawn together, which was about as expressive as he ever got.

At last Mom asked, "What does it all mean?"

"We're not certain," Mr. Kane said. "The investigation is ongoing."

"So what now?" Conryu asked. "I don't really want to spend my whole summer vacation locked up."

"I'm sorry, Conryu, but until we deal with whoever wants to kill you it's best if you stay here where it's safe." Mr. Kane offered an apologetic shrug. "Please understand it's not just you that's at risk. If another attack should happen someplace even more crowded, innocent bystanders might be injured. We must consider their safety as well."

That sucked, but Conryu understood his point. He'd have felt awful if anyone at the carnival had gotten hurt by monsters that were after him.

"There's another matter to consider," Mrs. Kane said.

"There is?" Conryu and his mom spoke at the same moment.

117

"Indeed. Your magical education is sorely lacking. The academy is set up With the expectation that all the incoming students Will have a certain base level of understanding. That is something you'll need to acquire in the next eight Weeks."

"Wait, summer vacation ends in ten Weeks, not eight."

"For first through tWelfth grade it does," Mrs. Kane said. "But for the academy and all the other colleges school starts early and ends late. Next year you'll only have six Weeks."

"Great." He glanced over at his mother Who Was positively beaming "You seem happy all of a sudden "

"This is perfect! You'll be safe inside studying and I Won't have to Worry, not With Shizuku's magic protecting you."

"Don't Worry." Maria took his hand under the table. "I can help you study. A refresher Will do me good."

"I'd be happy to help as Well," Mrs. Kane said. "Some of the later concepts are complex. I have a job next month that Will take me out of toWn for a Week, but other than that I'm at your serVice "

Conryu looked at the smiling faces staring at him and choked back a sigh. Eight Weeks of intensely studying a subject he couldn't care less about folloWed by four years of more studying it

Great

Chapter 5

Lady Raven

O rin reached the Department lobby and headed straight for the coffee machine. The secretaries hadn't arrived yet so he was forced to make a batch for himself. He yawned as the coffee dripped into the pot. At least it would be fresh; Orin seldom got a fresh cup of coffee at work.

He rolled his shoulders, trying to work the tension out of them. The murders and magical chaos were wearing on him. Not to mention he felt terrible about Conryu being stuck inside for his whole vacation. Maybe he could arrange some guards to watch him during a day trip or something.

To cap off his mountain of problems he'd promised the Department's full cooperation to the police commissioner on an early morning call Not that he had a ton of resources to offer. Despite the name, the Department of Magic only had four wizards on staff and only two of those were especially powerful.

The attacks had left the city on edge. In addition to keeping him safe, Orin hoped that if Conryu stayed out of sight it Would calm the public. The coffee stopped dripping and Orin poured himself a helping in a paper cup

"I'll have one as Well." Terra strolled over. She appeared fully recovered after her adventure at the carnival. Only a slight shadoW under her eyes betrayed any Weariness.

Orin handed her his cup and fixed himself another. He'd been so intent on his thoughts he'd never even noticed her come through the door. When they'd both taken a good long drink he asked, "Any neWs?"

"Not yet. Detective Chang is Working through statements taken from the carnival Workers, but Who knoWs hoW long that Will take and nothing may even come of it. There's nothing left of the spell that summoned the shadoW hounds so that's a dead end. I'm not sure Where to go next, Chief."

"Let the detective do his Work. When he has something I'm sure he'll let you knoW. MeanWhile, We have another test to administer. Is Clair in yet?"

"Her car Wasn't in her spot, but it's early." Terra finished her coffee and tossed the cup. "Are you really going to go through With this? I'm telling you she's not involved With the Society anymore."

"I trust you as much as I trust anyone outside my family and I still made you Wear the ring. Even if I didn't harbor doubts about Clair I'd make her do it, just to be safe."

"I'm not sure if I should be pleased by the compliment or annoyed by your stubbornness."

"Be pleased; your annoyance isn't going to affect my decision in the least."

She finally cracked a smile. "Fair enough. It's not like you're treating her any different than the rest of us. I'll let you know when she gets in."

Orin left Terra contemplating a second cup of coffee and headed up to his office. One good thing about getting in early, the halls were quiet.

"Orin!" a thick Scottish accent called from behind him.

He turned to find Angus marching toward him. Orin wanted to slam his head into the wall. So much for the quiet. "Let's go in my office and have a seat, Angus."

"Certainly, certainly." The professor followed Orin into his office and sat in the guest chair. "Is the boy okay? If anything happens to him my work will be ruined."

Orin slumped in his leather chair and blew out a sigh. Nice to see Angus had his priorities straight. If he never had to listen to another word about Angus's precious research it would be a fine thing. "Conryu isn't hurt and I'm sure he'll be thrilled to hear you were concerned. Was there anything else?"

Angus stared off into the middle distance. "It's the Aegis of Merlin. The great wizard's spirit is protecting his successor. This is more proof of my theory. Just watch, Orin. I'll be vindicated and all those who laughed at me will have to eat crow."

"If you say so. Now I have work to do."

"Oh yes, I remember what I wanted to ask you now. When can I talk to him again?"

Orin shrugged. "That's up to him. If Conryu wants to talk to you I don't care, but I'm not going to order him to."

"That's fine. Maybe I'll head over to your building later and try my luck."

Orin nodded. "Fine, just don't make a nuisance of yourself. Conryu's a good kid, but if he makes up his mind to, he's more than capable of throwing you out."

"I saw his display Saturday. I assure you I'll be on my best behavior."

Angus mercifully took his leave. Too bad he had to foist him off on Conryu, but getting the obsessed professor out of the office for the day would be a relief.

An hour later Orin was halfway through the weekend reports when Terra poked her head into his office. "She's here."

"Come in."

Terra and Clair stepped into his office and stood in front of his desk. Orin knew his wife and Clair had their differences, but he tried not to let it influence him.

"You wanted to see me, sir?" Clair adjusted her badge then tucked her hands inside her sleeves.

Orin took the ring of compulsion out of a locked drawer in his desk and held it up. "Everyone that knew about Conryu's press conference has been cleared of involvement in the attack except you. Put the ring on and state that you had nothing to do with the attack on Conryu."

"Is this because of my history?" Clair asked. "I assure you I haven't had anything to do with the Society since I graduated."

"Everyone did it, me included. I have to be sure, Clair. It's not personal." Orin slid the ring across his desk to her.

Clair looked at Terra, who nodded. She slipped the ring on. "I had nothing to do with the attack on Conryu Koda. I haven't been in contact with the Le Fay Society since I graduated from the academy."

Orin nodded, surprised and pleased that he Was Wrong about Clair. She took the ring off and handed it to him. "Thank you. I'm glad you didn't have anything to do With it. Unfortunately, noW I have no idea Who might have been behind the attempted murder"

"Oh, god." Clair's hand Went to her mouth. "There's one other person Who might have knoWn."

"Who?" Orin returned the ring to the locked draWer. He'd take it to storage later. "I questioned everyone that Was in the room When We decided to hold the press conference. I didn't even tell Maria and Shizuku about it beforehand. You Were the only other person outside the group Who kneW about Conryu and could have found out about the press conference"

"What about Mercia?"

"Who?" Orin couldn't for the life of him remember someone by that name

"The Wizard Who discovered Conryu. Mercia Bottomley, she's one of my testers. She Was in the room When We determined Conryu had Wizard potential and it Wouldn't have been difficult for her to learn about the press conference. The invitation Was sent through the unsecured server"

"I totally forgot about her," Orin said.

"As did I." Terra grimaced. "With everything that's happened I never gave her another thought after Orin sat her in that chair in the corner. She simply faded into the background."

"Mercia's good at that," Clair said.

"We need to speak to her at once." Orin stood up. "Where is she?"

"She called in sick this morning," Clair said. "I didn't think anything of it at the time, but now I don't know."

"Damn it! How could we have been so sloppy?" Orin paced and only the fact that he was bald kept him from pulling his hair out. "I assume her address is in her personnel file. You two get over there and bring her in. I don't care how sick she is."

* * *

The Department car raced down the narrow streets, dodging pedestrians and squealing around corners. Terra kept a white-knuckled grip on the handle above the passenger-side door. Sweat plastered her gray robe to her back. The broken air conditioning combined with Clair's driving had her drenched. Clair slammed on the brakes and cranked the wheel, fishtailing and screeching the tires of the sedan

Horrified onlookers stared for a moment before running for their lives. Terra knew just how they felt, but she didn't have anywhere to escape to. If they ever went out on an assignment together again there was no way Clair was driving, she could give Terra directions

"Would you slow down?" Terra said. "I'd like to make it there in one piece so we can bring Mercia in for questioning."

"Chief Kane said to hurry. Besides, I haven't had this much fun in years "

"I don't think he's in this big a rush, now slow down before you kill someone."

"Spoilsport. We're almost there anyway." Clair slowed to an only somewhat reckless speed and made a left down Bleak Street. Young men hung around in doorways, wearing tattered clothes and sometimes going shirtless to better display their tattoos. Scantly clad women, girls really, cuddled up against the thugs

"Are you sure this is where she lives?"

"We don't pay the testers very much, it's probably all Mercia can afford. Maybe that's why she betrayed us."

"She could have just asked for a raise," Terra said. "What are we looking at, power-wise?"

"Between three and four hundred. We only use the weakest wizards for testing, mostly because they can't do much else, magically speaking. She only works two days a week as it is, that's why I was surprised she called in sick. I had her scheduled for two more schools today"

Clair slammed on the brakes in front of a four-story tenement covered with graffiti, bringing them to a screeching halt. The designs painted on the walls appeared geometric and intricate, somewhat like magical runes, but their meaning was lost to Terra, assuming they had any meaning

They climbed out and locked the doors. Terra put her hand on the hood and chanted a simple warding spell. Anyone that tried to steal or vandalize their car would regret it.

"She's in Apartment C on the top floor." Clair headed for the rusty door

"Of course she is. What do you want to bet the elevator doesn't work?"

"Even if it does, I wouldn't use the elevator in a place like this"

Terra couldn't argue with that. The lock on the front door was missing and the glass had been smashed out. Not very secure, but then again there was probably nothing worth stealing inside.

Clair shoved the door open and after a quick search they found the stairs, steep narrow things made from rusty metal At least they didn't sway or rattle when Terra stepped on them Sometimes you had to be grateful for small favors

When they reached the top floor landing Terra was panting and her heart raced She really needed to get out of the office more and into the gym To make matters worse Clair didn't even seem out of breath

Terra straightened, determined not to show any weakness "Shall we?"

Clair nodded and the door whined when she pushed it open Crumpled-up newspapers, rotten food, and other things Terra didn't want to look too closely at littered the hall beyond God almighty, what a mess And the stink, ugh If this was the best a Department tester could afford, Terra would advise Orin to give them both a raise

Terra muttered a simple wind spell to circulate fresh air around her nose and mouth She took a deep breath of clean air Much better Clair continued on down the hall, seeming untroubled by the garbage

The younger wizard stopped in front of the third door and knocked "She's cast a simple ward Probably a prudent precaution given the neighborhood "

Terra nodded in silent agreement The city should tear the building down and start from scratch

A minute passed and no one answered the door Clair knocked again "Mercia! We need to talk to you "

Still nothing

"Do you want to break the ward or should I?" Clair asked

Terra motioned toward the door. "Be my guest."

Clair crossed the fingers of both hands then crossed her arms at the wrist. She spoke the first words of a basic magic negation spell and the hall grew darker. Liquid shadow gathered around Clair as she chanted. When she finished she threw both hands toward the door and uncrossed her fingers, releasing the gathered dark energy.

Her power lashed out, striking the ward and blowing it apart The light returned to normal and Clair reached out to push the door open. The moment she touched it the wood crumbled to shavings and the doorknob clattered to the floor.

She looked back at Terra, who shrugged. "You might have used too much energy "

"That was the weakest breaking spell I know."

"Your modulation needs work. You could have weakened the spell further by chanting softer or only crossing two fingers instead of all four. It doesn't matter. We can pay for a new door out of petty cash. Let's grab Mercia and get out of here."

Dim light filled the apartment. Heavy drapes covered the small windows and when Terra tried the switch nothing happened. She cupped her palm and whispered, "Light," summoning a glowing white globe.

The empty living room gave no clues about the woman living here. What sort of person didn't even have a chair and tv? The kitchen was just as empty as the living room. A single door on the opposite wall led, she assumed, to the apartment's lone bedroom. If Mercia was here that's where she had to be.

Terra went to the door and toed it open. The bedroom held a single, small end table situated right in the center. It was the first and only piece of furniture in the place Sitting in the center of the table was an undecorated gold ring

Terra reached for it then paused and spoke a simple detection spell The ring registered as magical, but there was no trap She picked the ring up for a closer look It was smooth, with no visible runes That was fairly common if you didn't want the world to know you had a magical item

"That's Mercia's She said it was her mother's wedding band "

"Unless her mother wore a magic ring I think we can safely assume that was bullshit Just like this address No one's lived here in a long time if ever I wonder if anything Mercia said on her employment form was the truth "

"What do you think it does?" Clair asked

Terra shook her head and pocketed the ring There was no way to know what it did until she returned to the lab and ran a proper analysis They went back toward the living room This whole trip was a waste of time The moment they passed through the bedroom door a tingle of power ran through Terra

A black energy field filled the door frame leading out into the hall Something moved in the darkness, almost like the fluttering of wings Identical energy fields covered the two small windows

"It's a trap!" Clair raised her hands and chanted a light barrier spell

Invisible energy swirled around them, ready to block anything that might present a threat For a moment nothing happened then the glow globe Terra had conjured winked out, plunging the apartment into complete darkness

She chanted the spell a second time, but the light energy Was sWalloWed the moment she summoned it. Terra froWned and sWitched to a fire spell. If she couldn't conjure light from her aligned element they Were in big trouble.

Terra's fire globe burned aWay some of the darkness, creating an oasis of light in the pitch-black room. She cast the spell a second time, brightening the room further Despite the increased light there Was nothing to see, only the bare floor and bare Wall. A deep snarl came from the bedroom, at least she thought it came from that Way. The light didn't extend far enough to reveal the doorWay.

"What Was that?" Clair asked.

"Nothing good, you can be certain. HoW did you do in combat training at the academy?"

"Middle of my class. Nothing outstanding. I took a job in the testing division because I thought I Wouldn't have to deal With situations like this."

"I transferred to R&D for the same reason. Looks like We're both going to be disappointed." Terra caught a hint of movement. At least she thought she did. It could have as easily been her imagination. "We need to go. Can you maintain the barrier While We move toWard the hall door?"

"I think so." Clair chanted again and the light flashed as the spell adjusted to its neW parameters. "We can move When you say "

A black form separated itself from the greater darkness. It looked vaguely humanoid, but lacked a face, and the body stretched beyond human proportions With long, skinny limbs ending in oversized claWed hands and feet.

The figure rushed toward them, claws extending as it drew closer. It lashed out, striking the light barrier and getting hurled back into the darkness.

"Was that what I think it was?" Clair's voice trembled.

"If you thought it was a Faceless One then yes." Terra marveled at how calm she sounded. There was a shadow demon out there trying to kill them and she managed to appear unconcerned

The Faceless One appeared out of the darkness again, slammed into Clair's barrier and was sent flying.

Clair groaned. "Every strike hurts me through the light I called. Its claws are tearing the barrier's essence apart and me along with it. How do we stop it?"

"I believe it's bound to the room. Once we're clear we can destroy it from a safe distance. Let's move." They eased closer to where Terra thought the door waited.

"What if it's not?"

"Then we may end up setting the creature free in the city. The danger's minimal since it's still morning, but once night falls all bets are off."

The Faceless One made another run at them and was again repulsed by the barrier. Clair's knees wobbled and Terra caught her before she fell

"One more of those and I'm done." Pain and exhaustion filled Clair's voice.

They were running out of time.

A moment later the door to the hall appeared in the light of Terra's fire globes. At least the door frame appeared. The opening Was filled With dark energy. Terra reached out to touch it and immediately jerked her hand back. It Would melt the flesh from their bones if they tried to force their Way out through that.

Their only chance Was to unravel the spell and she doubted the Faceless One Would give them the time.

"What's above us?" Terra asked.

"This is the top floor. There shouldn't be anything above us "

"Good." Terra chanted in the language of fire, sending more poWer to her fire globes.

The Faceless One attacked again and Was sent flying. The light died and Clair collapsed behind her. They Were defenseless noW.

Terra finished the spell and hurled the tWin balls of flame at the ceiling. They detonated on impact, bloWing a tWenty-foot hole in the ceiling. Bright morning sunlight shone doWn into the apartment, stabbing the Faceless One With golden shafts.

The shadoW demon threW its head back in a silent scream of pain. Its essence began to burn aWay at once. Terra sent streams of fire hammering into it to speed its dissolution. A minute later the creature Was gone, along With the darkness barriers over the remaining WindoW and hall door.

Terra glanced up at the hole she'd made. Some of the exposed timbers smoldered and several splintered ends burned With enthusiasm. She hissed and snapped her fingers, snuffing out the flames instantly.

Clair scrambled to her feet looking pale, but otherWise unharmed. "That Was too close."

Indeed it was. If Mercia had warded the ceiling as well as the windows and doorway their little adventure may have ended much differently.

"No three or four hundred power level wizard set up all this. Either Mercia had help or she pulled an even bigger one over on us than I first thought." Terra glared around the ruined living room.

They left the destroyed apartment and went out into the hall. Clair slumped against the wall while Terra dug out her phone. She needed to let Lin know what had happened. Hopefully he could convince his superiors this was connected to his case and she wouldn't need to deal with another cop.

* * *

Lady Raven stood in the center of her magic circle and adjusted the black raven mask so the eyeholes aligned properly. The shadowy casting chamber held nothing that might distract her. Even the smallest mistake when she was working on a project could mean her end. The upcoming meeting held similar risks. If she couldn't explain her actions to the Hierarchs' satisfaction she might easily end up dead

It was a shame she had to discard her Mercia persona. She'd gotten comfortable in that one over the last several years. She'd also gathered a great deal of information for her superiors. On the other hand she wouldn't miss having to show deference to those arrogant women at the Department. If they knew her true power they wouldn't have been so smug. Well, they knew it now. She smiled

When the simple ward she'd woven over the door to Mercia's apartment shattered she'd recognized the magic that broke it as belonging to her former superior at the Department. When the trap she'd left inside activated, Lady Raven assumed she would be down two enemies. To her surprise, Clair and Terra had managed to defeat her Faceless One. Those two were turning out to be tougher foes than she'd expected.

Their time would come, just like the abomination's time would come. She'd failed to kill the boy twice, but when the third time came he'd die just as surely as day turned to night.

Lady Raven tried to clear her mind of irrelevant thoughts. The time for the meeting drew near and her superiors would be able to sense any doubts and weakness. Like the animals whose masks they wore, the Hierarchs would attack at the slightest sign of weakness.

A tingle ran through the mask, prompting her to speak the activation spell, connecting her mind to the group. All around her the shadows seemed to flicker and flow, forming five shadowy avatars of the Hierarchs. Each wore a mask similar to hers. Directly in front of her was the Supreme Hierarch in her dragon mask. Flanking her, two per side, were wizards in animal masks. A tiger, lion, bear, and wolf. Beside the Hierarchs, one on each side, were two Sub-Hierarchs, a bluejay and a mockingbird. Either one of whom would be thrilled if Lady Raven fell flat on her face.

"Lady Raven," Lady Dragon said. "It has come to our attention that you have deviated from the plan. Is everything still on track?"

"Yes, Mistress. I only sacrificed the spare gem in hopes of killing the abomination."

"A task at which you failed " Lady Mockingbird made no attempt to disguise her glee

"Yes, I admit the boy survived, due to outside influences, but the other sites are secure and the authorities have no idea of their existence The plan will proceed with no issues "

"And the abomination?" Lady Tiger asked

"For now he is beyond my reach, but I have other tools that can deal with him when the time comes "

"No " Lady Dragon spoke with finality "Focus on your mission In time the boy will come out of hiding There is no need to rush "

"Yes, Mistress " It galled Lady Raven that she wouldn't have another shot at Conryu, but having failed twice perhaps it was for the best A third mistake would not be looked on favorably

"And, Lady Raven " Lady Dragon raised her hand, displaying the Scepter of Morgana for them all to see, a less than subtle reminder that in their true mistress's absence she ruled the Society "You have already lost your position in the Department Should you fail to carry the plan to fruition we will have no further use for you "

Lady Dragon vanished, followed quickly by the others, leaving Lady Raven alone in her casting chamber She pulled her mask off to be sure the connection was fully severed then fell, trembling, to her knees The chill of her mistress's disappointment sank deep into her bones

She couldn't fail again, not if she wanted to live

Lady Raven frowned and considered what her mistress had said She only commanded that Lady Raven herself not attack Conryu again It was possible the Hierarchs remained unaware that she'd prompted the zealot to attack the boy at his press conference

In that case it Wouldn't take much effort to convince a fresh batch of the fools to take another shot at him. She even kneW the perfect time.

* * *

Lin found Terra and her companion, a Wizard he hadn't met before, standing in the hall outside the smoking remains of an empty apartment. Inside, a team of firemen checked for hot spots or embers that might still be a threat. They'd evacuated the fifteen people in the building just to be safe. Considering the damage to the roof he doubted they'd be alloWed to stay in their homes tonight or any night until repairs Were completed.

The lack of smoke in the hall surprised Lin until he realized the Wizards had probably done something to keep it clear. They Wouldn't have Wanted to stand around coughing While they Waited for him.

"You tWo okay?"

Terra looked his Way and smiled. It surprised him hoW good that felt

"We're fine, Lin, thanks. Was anyone hurt in the blast?"

"EMTs are checking everyone out doWnstairs, but they seem fine. What happened?"

Terra told him about the trap and hoW they escaped. When she finished he asked, "What about your colleague? There Was no sign of her beyond the ring?"

"No, and I doubt she ever stayed in that apartment. I'm afraid We need to consider Mercia a suspect in the murders and the attack on Conryu."

Lin tried to smooth his suit and failed. "If you can send me a picture of her I'll put out a BOLO request."

"Of course, but Mercia can alter her appearance with a simple illusion so I don't know how much good it will do you." Terra shrugged her shoulders and worked her neck from side to side. If they'd been alone he would have offered her a massage. "Any luck with the carnival people?"

"No, they've left Sentinel City for wherever they go while they wait for the island to return to the west coast. I'm afraid they were just innocent people with the bad fortune to get mixed up in things that didn't concern them."

"I suspect you're right," Terra said. "It's a shame, but I don't think we could have done anything except what we did."

"Me neither, but that doesn't make it suck any less."

"No, it doesn't. If there's nothing else, Lin, we need to head back and analyze the ring."

"Of course." Lin and Terra shook hands. "Let me know what you find?"

"Will do." Terra guided her still-shaky companion down the hall and out of sight

Lin sighed. It was a shame Terra was a wizard. She would have made an excellent detective.

"Hey, Sarge," one of the firemen called from the apartment. He'd worked with the guy on an arson investigation a year ago and they'd kept in touch.

"What's up?"

"The room's clear. The wizard did a good job snuffing out all the hot spots. We're going to head out."

"Thanks, guys." Lin took his leave. Outside, one of the uniforms lifted the crime scene tape for him Lin climbed into his beat-up four-door and headed uptoWn. The techs had finished analyzing Mort Call's laptop and they traced the person he chatted With to an internet cafe at the edge of a middle-class neighborhood that bordered on a rougher area Hopefully they had security footage

Lin didn't bother With his siren as he Wove through the midday traffic. Hundreds of people going about their business Without a clue that an insane Wizard Was threatening the city. City Hall Wouldn't put it on the neWs unless they absolutely had to. The panic could end up being Worse than Whatever the Wizard had in mind

He turned off the main road and into a neighborhood of mixed residential and small businesses. The internet cafe Was at the edge of Cliff Street and barely hanging on given the spread of broadband and cellphones

Speaking of Which, Lin's phone buzzed in his pocket. He parked in front of the cafe and dug it out. It Was a text message from Terra With Mercia's picture. He'd seldom seen a more average-looking Woman save for the deep Wrinkles. She Wouldn't even need a disguise. Mercia could Walk doWn the street and never draW a second look.

Why couldn't anything be easy? If she had a hook nose, maybe a missing eye and some tattoos, anything to make her stand out Would help. Lin slid out of his car and Walked up to the cafe. They hadn't opened yet, but a young Woman With purple hair and studs running up the side of her ear Was fiddling With one of the computers. Lin rapped on the door until she looked up He pressed his badge to the glass

She hurried over and opened the door "Can I help you, Officer?"

Lin showed her the picture on his phone "Do you recognize this woman?"

"Sure, she gave me my wizard's test last year I failed "

"I was thinking more recently "

"Oh, then no, I guess not "

"Does this place have security cameras?" Lin asked

"These days every place does " The girl gave her hair a flip "We keep three days' worth You want to take a look?"

"Is it digital?"

"Yup "

"If I give you an address can you download the contents to the police server?"

"I can do better than that, I'll just swap the hard drives and you can take them with you Be a lot faster than downloading on our crappy connection "

Lin blinked, surprised at how helpful she was "That would be great, but won't your boss object?"

"Naw, he used to be a cop If I was anything but helpful he'd toss me out on my ear Just wait here and I'll bring you those hard drives "

"Thanks " Lin watched as she jogged back through the rows of computers and disappeared through an open doorway into the back room

The moment she was out of sight he tiptoed along behind her He stood in the doorway as she frantically tapped commands into a console tied to a server rack

"You wouldn't be trying to delete evidence, would you?"

She leapt back from the keyboard and looked frantically for an escape. The only way out was through Lin and he had his hand on his pistol grip.

"Please don't do anything stupid. I'd hate to have to shoot you."

"If I let you have those hard drives he'll kill me."

"Who, your boss? You said he used to be a cop."

She smiled and shook her head. "That wasn't the whole story."

"What is the whole story?"

"You have to get me out of the city. Promise me a ticket out of town and I'll tell you everything."

"Deal. May as well grab those hard drives while we're at it."

* * *

Lady Raven had barely finished posting on the fanatics' secure forum when someone banging on the door got her attention. She typed a short command that disconnected her and erased her browser's cache so no one could see what she'd been doing.

She turned to look and found a man in his forties wearing a rumpled blue suit standing in front of the door. He pressed a badge to the glass. Damn it to hell! How had the police found this place already?

It was inevitable that they would, but she'd hoped to get another month or two out of it. Worse, if they'd found the cafe it was only a matter of time before the Skulls came to their attention. The bikers knew far too much for her own good. They were useful tools, but it seemed they had played their parts. It was time to cut them loose.

A plan formed as she made her way to the door. By the time she unlocked it and invited the cop inside she knew exactly what she had to do. It was a small miracle he hadn't arrived ten minutes earlier. If she'd had to send the message to the zealots from her own computer it would have been far riskier. So risky in fact that she might not have even bothered

"Can I help you, Officer?"

The cop showed her a picture of herself on his phone. "Do you recognize this woman?"

It took all her willpower not to laugh. After a brief interrogation during which Lady Raven did her best to be as helpful as possible, helpful enough to make him suspicious, she went to the back room to retrieve the hard drives.

The moment she left his line of sight she darted to her station at the servers and typed commands that would automatically delete everything she didn't want the authorities to know about. Which was pretty much everything but the contents of three hard drives she'd set up for this exact eventuality.

"You wouldn't be trying to delete evidence, would you?"

As she'd hoped, his suspicious nature prompted him to follow her. She looked left and right, trying her best to appear frightened and desperate, a scared girl caught out of her depth Lady Raven had honed her acting skills over years of undercover work. In truth she'd spent so much time pretending to be other people she'd almost forgotten who she started out as.

"Please don't do anything stupid. I'd hate to have to shoot you."

His pitiful weapon couldn't have harmed her unless she allowed it to, but she cowered like the girl she appeared to be. She blamed her fear on the dupe that ran the shop for her He tried to be reassuring and she let him calm her doWn. They struck a bargain and she pulled the three hard drives she Wanted him to have in the first place. It Was so much easier to convince someone to do What you Wanted When they thought it Was their idea.

The cop packed her and the hard drives into the back seat of a car that had seen better days. He jumped in the front and they drove aWay. Lady Raven kept her hands hidden as she Wove a Wind spell that Would carry a message to Iron Skull. By the end of the day her dupe Would be at the bottom of the ocean.

She smiled as they made their Way to the police station. What better place to hide than right under their noses?

* * *

Lin guided the purple-haired tech doWn the hall toWard an empty interrogation room. He glanced doWn at the chipped, filthy black and White tile floor. The station needed to invest in an extra janitor. The mess that Was the main corridor from the front of the station to the rear didn't fill a person With confidence about the quality of people Working for the city police. A light buzzed and flickered overhead as the bulb sloWly died, adding to the ambiance

"This place reminds me of a mental Ward from a loW-budget horror film."

Lin Wanted to argue, but he had nothing. "Try not to judge the police by the station. There are a lot of good people Working here. We do our best With limited resources."

"Hey, Sarge." One of the guys from sex crimes, a three-hundred-pound heap of blubber named Louie that seldom left the office, Waved him over to his desk in the maze of cubicles.

"Wait here." Lin left his witness and walked over. "What's up?"

"Got a message from that Cullen guy that owns the carnival. One of his people got so depressed she killed herself."

"What?"

"Yeah, the guys investigating wanted me to let you know since it dovetails with your investigation."

"Thanks, Louie. I'll bring you a Bear Claw tomorrow."

"Fuck you, Chang."

They shared a good-natured grin and Lin went back to his witness. "Sorry for the wait."

She shrugged. "What else have I got to do? Anything exciting?"

"Another body. It seems I'm drowning in them lately. At least this one didn't stand up and start walking around. Come on, I'll get you settled then send those hard drives down to the tech department. It shouldn't take our facial recognition system long to see if my suspects visited your cafe "

"You're going to see a lot more than that."

Lin raised his hand. "Please, don't say anything until we reach the interrogation room. Once we're inside everything will be recorded. That way we avoid any misunderstandings."

Fifteen minutes later Lin sat across from the witness in a dingy, bare room. A single light bulb flickered over their heads. The chipped plastic table between them looked like a reject from a condemned school. Behind the two-way mirror Lin's boss, Captain Connor, watched and listened. He was as eager to crack this case as Lin and had agreed to allowing the girl a deal for anything short of murder

"State your name for the record, please," Lin said

"Lacy Winn."

"Again, for the record, you have the right to an attorney during this deposition. Do you Waive that right?"

"I do." Her voice sounded steady despite the circumstances. Lacy Was clearly a tough girl.

"Okay. Tell us your story."

"Six months ago I took a job doing basic maintenance on the cafe's computers. The job came With a little hole-in-the-Wall apartment upstairs. I didn't get good enough grades to qualify for college, not even one of the tWo-year places. At first it seemed like a sWeet deal, but then all these strange guys started coming and going early in the morning and late at night."

"Strange guys?" Lin asked. "Please be more specific."

"I can't give you names, if that's What you mean. They didn't exactly introduce themselves. They Were big, biker-looking guys. You knoW, lots of leather and spikes. Not to mention knives and guns. Five of them shoWed one night With enough firepoWer to start a War. Scared the hell out of me."

"Illegal Weapons?"

"They had clips as long as my arm. That seems like the sort of thing you guys Would froWn on."

"What about the tattoos, or patches on their jackets? Anything that could give us an idea Who We're dealing With."

She thought for a moment. "There Were a lot of skulls. Skull patches, skull tattoos, one guy had a helmet that looked like a skull. They all Wore rings that looked like barbed Wire. Does that help?"

Lin smiled and tried to look encouraging "It all helps You said we'd see a lot on the recordings What did you mean by that?"

Lacy cleared her throat "Can I have a drink?"

"Sure " Lin pushed himself out of the chair, poked his head out into the hall, and spotted a uniformed officer walking down the hall "Excuse me Would you get my witness a glass of water?"

The officer pulled a face, but nodded "Yes, Detective "

Lin went back inside and sat down "It'll just be a minute Do you want to keep going while we wait or do you need a break?"

"I can keep going Like I said, they scared me so I reset the security cameras to run during off hours when the bikers were there Sort of an insurance policy It reacts to movement so the camera doesn't record all the time and I partitioned the hard drive to keep it from automatically erasing with the rest of the data The light isn't great, but you should be able to make out all of them, at least a little "

"Clever girl "

The door opened and the officer came in with a plastic cup of water He set it on the table, nodded once, and silently marched out Didn't look like he and Lin would be best friends anytime soon

"Tell me about your boss "

Lacy set the cup down and wiped a drop of water off her lips "Mr Connelly? I don't know much about him He doesn't spend a lot of time at the cafe It's more of an investment for him Not an especially good one nowadays either "

"Is there anything else you can think of that might be valuable to us? Even the smallest detail could be vital "

"I'm sorry. I don't really know much. It's not like we're pals or anything. I was just a nobody that kept the computers running"

"Okay. Thank you, Lacy." Lin held out his hand and they shook. "Two officers will take you to a department safe house. As soon as we finish going over the drive and we're sure we don't have any more questions, I'll take you to the airport myself."

Half a minute later Captain Connor and two uniforms stepped into the room. Lacy went with the uniforms leaving Captain Connor and Lin alone in the room

"What do you think?" Connor asked.

Lin shook his head. "Until we know what's on the tape we only have her word to go on. Certainly nothing I'd want to take to court"

"What's your gut tell you?"

"That she's telling us everything she knows, but that there's a lot more going on here than we know about." Lin picked up the plastic cup by the lip. "I'm going to have this dusted for prints and see what else we can learn about Miss Winn."

* * *

Conryu turned the page of the two-inch-thick book Mr. Kane had given him before they left last night. It was the current edition of The Basics of Wizardry and it was written in the most dry, boring voice Conryu had ever read. He knew they didn't put much effort into making textbooks entertaining, but god almighty it was like the author went out of her way to make this one dull

Maybe she considered it some sort of test If you didn't have the focus and discipline to make it through the book you wouldn't make it as a wizard That was the most charitable explanation he could come up with

Unable to stand it anymore, Conryu slammed the cover shut and tossed the book on the couch He switched on the tv Maybe he could find a replay of last night's ballgame The clock on the mantle read ten in the morning He should be out doing something, anything, not cooped up like an inmate He flipped to one of the news channels and there was his face

"Who is the real Conryu Koda?" the hostess asked "The first ever confirmed male wizard, Conryu comes from an unremarkable background "

He switched it off What the hell did she know about the real him? He'd never even met the woman Well, when you had twenty-four hours of news to fill you had to talk about something Conryu hopped out of the recliner and went to the kitchen Some junk food would take his mind off wizards and reporters He pulled the refrigerator door open and scanned the awful selection of fruits and vegetables Where was that last piece of lasagna?

Someone knocked and Conryu closed the fridge Thank goodness That had to be Maria Maybe she'd summarize the book for him Knowing her she'd read it cover to cover more than once

He peeked out into the hall just to be sure and frowned at the mass of wild white hair He knew that hair, but what was that crazy professor doing here?

Conryu opened the door a crack and frowned out at the old man "Are you lost?"

"No, in fact I was hoping we could talk a bit. I have so many questions. May I come in, please?"

Conryu looked from the professor, to the book on the couch, and back again. Which was the lesser evil? Finally he decided it was a toss up, but he didn't want to offend one of Mr. Kane's colleagues.

He pulled the door open the rest of the way. "You have half an hour, then I need to get back to studying."

The professor, McSomething, Conryu couldn't remember the rest, hustled into the apartment and looked around like he'd never seen one before.

"Looking for something in particular?" Conryu asked.

"Sorry. I was just trying to understand how the most amazing person ever born could come from such an ordinary place This might be any one of ten thousand apartments in this city. It's inexplicable."

"Yeah. I won't tell my mom you said that as she's quite proud of her decorating." Conryu plopped down into the recliner. "So what do you want, Professor?"

"Angus, please." The professor sat beside the book on the couch. "I've been doing genealogical research on both sides of your family and you know, there isn't a single wizard on either side as far back as I could find records. Would you be willing to give me a blood sample so I can check your DNA for anomalies?"

"No." Angus blinked at his abrupt answer. Conryu didn't especially care. He had no intention of being poked, prodded or tested any more if he could avoid it. "What does my family history have to do with it?"

"Don't you know anything about magic?" Angus pressed on before he could say the sarcastic remark that popped into his head "Wizards tend to run in families Not always as directly as your friend Maria, with daughter following mother, but all wizards can find another wizard somewhere in their ancestry, except you "

"How far back did you go?" Conryu asked He didn't really want to get in to this, but now his curiosity had been roused

"Things become murky after ten generations on your mother's side, but I traced your father's family all the way back to the second generation after the Elf War, and not a speck of magic could be found It's absolutely astonishing "

"Huh Well, was there anything else?"

"Could you tell me what it felt like when you touched the testing device? Did you get a thrill of power when you learned you were a wizard?"

Thrill of power? This guy read too many comic books "I didn't feel anything, Professor, except my dreams dying You seem to be the one getting a thrill out of my problems, but for me they're nothing but a pain in the ass I have to delay starting my job for four years, study a subject that doesn't interest me in the least, all while hopefully not getting killed by any of the nuts that object to my existence Mr Kane said that once I finish my training at the academy I'll be free to do what I want And what I want is to have as little to do with magic as possible "

"No! Don't you see? You have a great destiny ahead of you You can't simply fade into obscurity You'll be famous the world over, the most powerful wizard ever You'll consult with kings and emperors just like your predecessor, Merlin You'll be a living legend and I'll be vindicated "

Conryu leapt to his feet, marched to the door and yanked it open "You and Merlin can both take a flying leap Now get out before I throw you out "

"Please, I have many more questions."

"I'm going to count to five and if you're still here I'll make you wish you weren't. And I promise you I won't need magic to do it. One!"

Angus scrambled to his feet.

"Two!"

He rushed across the living room, out the door, and stopped in the hall. "If you change your—"

Conryu slammed the door in his face and leaned against it. He didn't know what was worse, the people that wanted to kill him or the ones that wanted to use him. At least the killers didn't try and pretend it was for his benefit.

Consult with kings and emperors. Ha! What in the world would he have to tell a king? Maybe if something broke on the royal motorcycle he could help, but his expertise ended there.

A knock sounded on the door. Stubborn old fart couldn't take a hint.

He yanked the door open and found Maria standing there stunning as ever, in a pale blue dress.

"Everything okay?" She shied away from him and Conryu realized he was still scowling like he expected the professor.

He smoothed his expression and stepped aside to let her enter. "Sorry. I had an unpleasant visitor and I was afraid he'd come back."

"Oh?"

He recounted what the professor had to say. When he finished he added, "I wasn't eager to renew the conversation."

"You really don't want to have anything to do with magic?"

Conryu groaned. Not Marla too.

149

Chapter 6

The Black Skulls

Terra sat in her cramped office surrounded by books of magic both neW and old. Despite its small size she Was most at home tucked aWay out of sight. Terra Wasn't good With people. She kneW she tended to be abrupt and to assume others Were as informed about magical matters as her. She'd fought the problem since her time at the academy and still hadn't beaten it.

Lin said he'd call around midmorning and she Was anxious to hear What he'd come up With. Who Was she kidding? Terra just Wanted to talk to him again. She felt like a teenager Waiting for some boy to call after their first date.

TWo days had passed since she last spoke to the detective though it seemed like longer. Unlike most people she dealt With outside the Department, Terra found the good detective easy to talk to.

For her part, she and Clair had figured out What the ring did: it Was a poWer suppressor. Mercia Wasn't a Weak Wizard after all. Unfortunately, they had no idea hoW great her true poWer

151

was. Though based on the trap she set at her fake apartment Terra guessed she was at least as strong as Shizuku and perhaps a little stronger

They also had no idea why she decided to hide her power in the first place. Clearly she wanted access to the Department without drawing any attention. As a tester Mercia would have known the names of every new student going to the academy, but that wasn't exactly secret information. The academy made enrolled students' names public. The government had determined that regular citizens had a right to know if they were dealing with a wizard.

Terra had made her report to Chief Kane yesterday and he had someone searching the academy records to try and find Mercia's true power level, but so far they'd found nothing, not even her name. The government kept meticulous records when it came to wizards, so the fact that they found nothing about Mercia was odd if not downright sinister. It seemed like every time they took a step forward it was followed by two more back.

Her phone rang, jarring Terra out of her contemplations. She could do nothing about the records so she needed to focus on things within her control, like figuring out who had attacked Conryu

She picked up the receiver. "Terra Pane."

"This is Detective Chang, Terra. We've made some progress in our investigation. I tracked the person chatting with Mort Call to an internet cafe. It seems a gang called the Black Skulls was using it as a meeting place. Since he hasn't woken up yet, is there any way you can extract information from Mr. Call's mind? Our wizard says it's possible, but beyond her ability."

"A psychic probe, it's not something I have any skill with, but my boss's wife might be able to do it. I'll ask him and let you know. Now, who are the Black Skulls and what do they have to do with Conryu and Mercia?"

"The Skulls are a biker gang that's into drugs and guns. They've also moved into illicit magical items. We have them on tape collecting mundane-looking items from an unknown individual. Our wizard found traces of magical energy at the cafe "

Terra frowned. She knew a little about the underground trade in magical items, but it tended to be narrow and limited to collectors. It didn't seem like the sort of thing that would interest a gang. "Would it be possible for me to have a look at the cafe? We have an amplification device that can give more information about those trace energies you found "

"Certainly. I'd prefer to speak to you in person anyway. Can you meet me there in an hour?" Lin gave her the address.

"I'll be there." She hung up and left her office.

It was a short walk down to the secure storage room. She'd been taking the stairs for the last two days to get a little exercise. Studying the energy patterns and chatting with Lin should be simple enough, no need to bring Clair along

She reached the thick steel door and placed her hand on a metal plate beside it. Terra spoke a brief incantation, deactivating the wards and unlocking the door. Inside the store room dozens of shelves held hundreds of items: books, scrolls, and other magical paraphernalia

Terra selected a set of glasses held together with silver wire. They would magnify the aura of any residual magic a hundred times. She reached for a silver ring, paused, then grabbed it. A little extra protection was never a bad idea. She slipped the ring on and headed for her car, locking the door behind her.

* * *

Terra found Lin leaning against his car waiting for her when she arrived. The internet cafe was a rundown dump sealed off with yellow police tape. She'd never had much use for technology. It tended to be more of a distraction than anything as far as she was concerned anyway.

Terra parked her beat-up car behind Lin's equally beat-up sedan. She didn't know where all her tax dollars were spent, but it wasn't on vehicles for public servants.

Lin opened her door for her, prompting a smile. "Thanks. Did your wizard mention what sort of magic she found?"

Lin opened his notebook. "Fire and darkness, both extremely weak."

"The residual aura might be weak, but whatever left them had to be reasonably strong or she would have found no trace at all." Terra strode toward the cafe door. "I'll know more shortly."

"Do you need the area clear or can I join you?"

"Join me, by all means. Your presence will make no difference one way or the other." She smiled and opened the door. "For the spell. I'll be glad for the company."

He smiled back and her heart did a little flutter. What was wrong with her? She was acting like a silly girl. When the door closed behind Lin she slipped the glasses on and chanted

"Reveal all things hidden "

Three dark trails appeared between the dingy rows of computers. "Darkness magic for sure."

Terra followed the trails toward the back of the cafe, bumping into chairs as she focused on the magic instead of where she was walking. Lin gently took her elbow and guided her around the various obstacles. The trails led to a blank wall. She touched the smooth, painted surface

"There's something hidden behind here."

"Are you sure? Our Wizard didn't mention even seeing anything in this part of the building "

Terra traced a square on the wall, leaving a glowing path behind. "Right here. I can't say what, but something was here, something powerful."

"Step back." Lin pulled a folding knife out of a coat pocket.

Terra moved aside and Lin stabbed the wall, cutting the wall board around the square she marked. When he finished he pulled the chunk of material out and tossed it on the floor. On the other side was a small niche built into the framing. Runes had been burned into the wood. The whole thing seethed with residual dark energy.

"Something potent was stored here at one time. Those are runes of containment and binding. Whoever used this hiding place didn't want whatever they put here leaking out."

"Can you tell what it was?" Lin asked.

Terra shook her head. "The residual energy doesn't have any real shape. Where did your Wizard detect the auras?"

"In the back room where they held their secret meetings. Through the door on your left "

Terra slipped through the door. The filthy office lit up with lines of darkness and fire. The dark magic was the same as whatever was in the niche. She scanned the walls and found a faint aura on the wall that was opposite the hole they just cut in the wall.

"Someone used magic to reach through the wall and retrieve whatever was stored there. The magic looks very similar to what we found at the carnival, only stronger. I can't tell much about the fire magic, but given what you said about the people gathered here I feel pretty confident it was a weapon. What sort of items were they trading?"

Lin consulted the ever-present notebook. "Five boxes and what looked like a glove."

"The glove is almost certainly the weapon, probably a Flame Hand Gauntlet, very dangerous. The five boxes I'm not sure about. The lines continue out the back door." Terra followed the dark energy outside. "They split up here, going in five different directions The trail dissipates after a hundred yards or so "

"So whatever was in those boxes could be anywhere."

Terra took her glasses off and returned them to their case. "I'm afraid so. When was the tape made?"

"Four nights before the attack on Conryu."

"That's a day before anyone even knew the boy had wizard potential. Whatever we've stumbled into is about far more than Conryu. That's a long time for such potent magical items to be in the hands of people who have no idea how to use them properly."

"We need to find the Skulls and learn what they did with them "

"Absolutely." Terra chewed her thumbnail and frowned. "The real question is: What, if anything, does all this have to do with Conryu and Mercia?"

"Even if it has nothing to do with them, I can't risk criminals having access to dangerous magic The threat to the city is too great "

* * *

The deep roar of Iron Skull's bike fell silent When he pulled into a parking spot outside Sentinel Central Hospital. He took off his helmet and hung it on the handlebars. The bone-White skull-shaped helmet alWays made him smile. It Was a gift from Mistress Raven. She said it Was an actual demon skull and it did alWays make him feel poWerful When he Wore it, though not as poWerful as his neW toy. He clenched his right fist, making the heavy leather of his gauntlet crunch. The pentagram on the back of his hand gloWed With an inner fire.

When she first gave him the magic glove Iron Skull couldn't believe it. He'd oWned and used all sorts of Weapons, but a magic flamethroWer, hoW fuckin' aWesome Was that? There had been a time When he could never have imagined calling anyone master, but serving Mistress Raven had become the single most fulfilling thing he'd ever done. The fact that she usually Wanted him to do all the things he liked best anyWay helped.

Take this morning. He got a message telling him to off Mort Call. Skull had no idea Who the fuck Mort Call Was and he didn't care. She Wanted him dead and Skull liked nothing better than killing people, especially noW that he had his flamethroWer. He'd already come up With a handful of neW Ways to kill people With it and he Was eager to try out his most recent idea. He'd burned that fat prick that ran the computer place to ashes, but that had ended too quick for him to really enjoy it.

Skull straightened his mohaWk and adjusted his black leather jacket, trying in vain to look less intimidating. Not that he had anything against killing everyone in the hospital if that's What it took to get Call, but Mistress Raven had made it clear that when she sent him to kill someone, ideally, he would only kill that one person. A massacre drew more attention than she wanted just now.

He checked his appearance in his bike's polished chrome gas cap. Not bad. He smiled, revealing a jumble of crooked yellow teeth. Skull gave his bike an affectionate pat and headed toward the main entrance. The huge, sprawling complex covered half a square mile if you counted the grounds. He'd need directions if he wanted to avoid searching all day for his mark.

Halfway to the door Skull spotted a man in his late fifties carrying a bouquet of flowers coming from his left. That was handy. Skull had almost reached him when the guy looked his way. The suit's eyes went wide then closed the instant Skull's fist sank into his gut. The guy slumped and Skull helped himself to the flowers.

Perfect. Now he really looked like a proper friend making a visit to his ailing buddy. Skull left the barely conscious man curled up in the fetal position and groaning on the sidewalk. What a wuss. Couldn't even take one punch to the gut.

The automatic doors opened at his approach. Inside was a waiting room filled with sick or injured people. A row of nurses sat behind a long desk, each at her own computer station. All but one was helping someone already. Skull ambled up to the free nurse, a dusky-skinned woman with cornrows and too much eye shadow. She flinched when she noticed Skull looking down at her

He smiled, trying to set her at ease. The way her eyes widened suggested he failed. "I'm here to visit an old friend of mine, Mort Call. Can you tell me which room he's in?"

"One moment, sir." The nurse typed, froWned at her screen, and typed something else. At last she looked up. "I'm sorry, Mr. Call is in police custody and isn't alloWed any visitors. If it's any consolation he Woke from his coma this morning. The doctors think his chances of recovering are good."

Skull didn't think his chances Were so good, and a pair of cops Wasn't going to improve them much. At least noW he kneW Why Mistress Raven Wanted him dead. If he kneW something and had Woken up it Was only a matter of time before he spilled his guts

"Maybe I could just go up and drop his floWers off. The cops could look them over and take them into the room. That Wouldn't hurt, right?"

The nurse finally smiled. "I suppose not. He's in room 560 in building C "

She gave Skull directions and he set off draWing the gazes of everyone in the Waiting room. Building C Waited a five-minute Walk from the main entrance. He passed doctors, nurses, janitors, and other visitors on his Way and Without fail they all did a double take When he strode past.

Skull shook his head and stepped into the elevator that Would take him to the fifth floor. He didn't look that unusual, did he? He kneW a lot of guys With a mohaWk and leather jacket. Maybe it Was the tattoos. He had a shattered skull pierced With a dagger inked on the side of his neck. It Was pretty hardcore. Though he had a trio of nastier ones on his chest

The elevator chimed and the doors slid open. An older couple took a step back When they saW him inside the elevator. Of all the people he encountered, the elderly seemed to react like that the most consistently. He held the door for them and they scurried in without a word of thanks. So much for the older generation having better manners

Skull walked to the nearest hall and checked the first room number he came to: 502. At the far end a pair of boys in blue sat in stiff chairs and sipped from paper cups. He grinned and stalked towards them. As he walked, Skull sent his thoughts into the gauntlet, drawing out the fire spirit's power the way Mistress Raven had taught him. When the back of his hand grew warm he knew it was ready.

He was almost to the room when one of the cops hopped to his feet and raised a hand. "I'm sorry, sir. No one is allowed to visit this patient"

"But I brought him flowers." Skull held out the bouquet. "Can't you at least give these to him?"

When the cop was only three feet away Skull lashed out, driving his gauntlet-covered fist into the cop's gut and releasing a blast of fire. Bright orange flames burst out his back and the cop collapsed

Skull caught him and hurled the dead cop at his still-living partner. The corpse caught the second cop halfway out of his chair. He scrambled to avoid it, but the weight of the body drove him back down.

Skull rushed over, grabbed the living cop's head and poured fire into it. The cop's skull burst like a ripe melon. That was always good for a laugh.

An alarm sounded and sprinklers sprang to life, drenching the hall. Skull stepped into Mort's room and found his target struggling to sit up with his hand cuffed to the bed rail.

Mort stared at him with wide, frightened eyes. "Who are you?"

"No one special."

Skull lunged across the room and slapped his gauntleted hand across Mort's mouth. He called on the magic again, sending flames down the mark's gullet, incinerating his internal organs. When he finished, smoke was literally coming out of Mort's ears.

Skull couldn't stop grinning. That had worked even better than he'd hoped. The only problem was when you burned up their lungs the target couldn't scream. Maybe next time he'd burn up some less vital organs and leave the target to die slowly.

Then again, if Mistress Raven wanted someone kept quiet, letting them die slowly might not be the way to go. Skull would just have to try it on one of his own victims. Maybe he'd grab someone on the way home. The guys would probably enjoy the show, take their minds off Numb getting his dumb ass killed.

Skull left the still-smoking corpse of Mort Call smoldering in his bed and stepped out into the hall. Voices shouted and nurses hustled patients and visitors toward the stairwell. It didn't look like they'd made it this far or noticed the dead cops yet. Skull considered dragging the bodies into Mort's room, but dismissed the idea at once. It would only delay the inevitable by a few minutes at best.

He stepped over the bodies, doing his best to ignore the streams of water plastering his mohawk flat against his head, and headed for the elevator. He pressed the call button, but it didn't light up. Annoyed now, he stabbed it three more times.

"Sir." A big, broad-shouldered orderly in purple scrubs spotted him and walked over. "The elevators are disabled during a fire emergency. You'll have to take the stairs."

"Of course they are " Skull shook his head That was the problem with hospitals, too safety conscious

A gasp from the orderly drew Skull's attention back to him He was staring down the hall at the dead cops Too bad, he seemed like a nice-enough guy On the other hand Skull never passed up a chance to use his gauntlet

The orderly looked away from the bodies just in time to catch a heavy fist to his forehead At the moment of impact Skull released a burst of fire The orderly's head exploded in a shower of blood and flames

Skull grinned That was the coolest fuckin' thing ever

A feminine scream from down the hall caught his attention A pretty redheaded nurse stood trembling, her hands to her mouth, staring at him He stomped down the hall toward her, ignoring the scattering of people headed for the stairs

Skull clamped his bare hand around the back of her neck "Shame you had to see that Now, we're going to walk out of here together Give me any trouble and I'll pop your head like a zit, got it?"

She managed a silent nod

Skull guided her toward the stairwell where they merged with the flow of people coming from the floors above It wasn't a particularly speedy group considering they were evacuating a fire Maybe they thought it was just a drill Of course all the people with canes and walkers didn't hurry things up any

The faint whine of sirens approaching reached him Sounded like the fire department was taking it seriously The sirens also convinced the healthier people to step on it and several jostled Skull in their haste to flee Remembering Mistress Raven's lecture about self-control, Skull refrained from burning them all to death

At the bottom of the stairs people were streaming out the nearest door. For his part Skull turned down the hall that led to the main entrance where he'd left his bike.

"Please don't hurt me," the nurse whispered.

Skull loved it when they begged. It made him want to hurt her even more. Looked like he wasn't going to have to grab someone on his way home. He'd just take—Skull glanced down at her name tag—Janice home with him.

The main waiting area had cleared out by the time they arrived. Through the glass doors four cop cars were visible. Each car had a pair of cops behind it pointing their guns at the entrance. How the hell did they know where he was going?

"Where are all the cameras in this dump?" When Janice didn't answer Skull gave her a shake. "Answer me."

"Everywhere." The word came out more of a whimper.

Great, the cops were probably watching him right now. He looked around until he spotted one of the cameras and flipped it off. Skull had hoped to make this a quick in and out, but it looked like he'd get to have a bit more fun before the day was done

Skull forced Janice directly in front of him and marched her closer to the door so the cops could take a good look. If there was one thing you could count on it was a hostage keeping the boys in blue honest. If they so much as farted in his direction Skull would burn her to death.

"We have you surrounded." Some asshole must have found a bullhorn. "Come out with your hands up."

They always said that Skull looked down at the now-crying Janice "Do you think that line ever works?"

"I don't know"

"Me either, but it's not going to work today" Skull pushed her close enough to trigger the automatic doors "Clear the fuck out of here or Janice is going from the hospital to the morgue"

A little whimper escaped the captive nurse It was a nice touch, but he doubted the cops heard her

"There's nowhere you can go," the asshole with the bullhorn said "Release the girl before someone gets hurt"

Skull shook his head "These cops need to catch a clue There're already four dead guys upstairs"

No comment from Janice She was probably overwhelmed by all the excitement

Skull raised his gauntleted hand and called the fire A stream of flame streaked toward the car nearest where he'd left his bike

The cops behind it scrambled to get clear

A moment later the gas tank exploded, sending the car up into the air before it came crashing down on its roof He adjusted his aim and commanded the fire to come forth again

* * *

Lin led Terra out of the cafe and toward their cars She really was a remarkable woman, strong, smart and dedicated If she worked for the police department he would have been delighted to have her for a partner

Terra took a deep breath and stretched "So what now?"

"I need to focus on finding the Skulls I wish I could help you find your missing wizard, but the gang represents a direct threat to the city and so gets priority"

Terra Waved off his apology. "I understand. Finding Mercia is the Department's responsibility anyWay. What about Conryu? Chief Kane has him basically on lockdoWn, but that Won't last forever. At the very least he'll have to leave his building to start school "

"KnoWing Conryu he Won't last seven Weeks cooped up inside. The truth is, and I'm reluctant to say this after my earlier mistake, I doubt there's an active effort being made to go after Conryu. As far as I can tell Mort acted alone and the incident at the carnival noW looks more like an attack of opportunity."

"That suggests if another opportunity should present itself he might still be in danger "

Before Lin could respond his phone rang. "Excuse me."

"Mort Call has been murdered at the hospital along With his guards," the police secretary said

"What? You're sure?"

"What is it?" Terra asked.

He held up a finger.

"We're sure. The attacker matches the description of one of your gang members. They have him surrounded. Since you're the officer of record for the case they asked me to let you knoW."

"I'm on my Way." Lin disconnected. "We're in luck. One of the Skulls is trapped in Sentinel Central Hospital. The guys are moving in noW to apprehend him."

"I'll come With you. If it's the one With the Flame Fist Gauntlet you'll need my help to subdue him."

"Climb in, I'll drive."

They loaded up and Lin took off at full speed, siren blaring. It only took five minutes to reach the hospital. The smoke Was visible after three minutes and the flames after four. Lin followed the smoke to the main entrance. Two police cars were burning. Beside the doors a man with a mohawk held a woman hostage. On his right hand he wore a glowing gauntlet.

The biker pointed the gauntlet at a third car. Terra lowered her window and began to chant in a hissing, sibilant language.

A ball of fire shot from the biker's glove.

Terra snapped her fingers and pointed. The fireball fizzled out halfway to the car.

Lin swerved to a stop behind the two intact vehicles. Terra never took her eyes off the biker and never stopped the chanting. She climbed out of the car and marched straight toward him. One of the uniforms rushed to stop her.

"It's okay." Lin waved him off. "She's a government wizard assisting in the investigation "

Terra snapped and pointed again. Lin looked away from the patrolman as the last sparks of the fireball sputtered in the air ten feet from the cars. She took another step forward.

"Don't go too close," the patrolman said. "He's holding a hostage "

Terra stopped moving, but continued chanting in that strange language. A twenty-foot wall of flame roared to life in front of the biker. Even from a distance the heat made Lin flinch.

There was movement then a figure staggered, screaming, through the flames. It was the nurse and her uniform had caught on fire.

"Don't shoot!" Lin shouted. "It's the hostage. Keep your eyes open for the perp "

Terra snapped her fingers a third time and the flames covering the Woman vanished. She raised her voice and the cadence of the chant sped up. Terra threW her hands to the side and the Wall of flame disappeared.

She bleW out a breath and fell silent. Lin rushed to check on the nurse. No sign remained of the biker.

The nurse had first- and second-degree burns on her hands and face, but the damage Wasn't anyWhere near as bad as it might have been if Terra hadn't been there.

"Are you alright, miss?" Lin asked

She nodded, tears streaming doWn her face. "I thought he Was going to kill me."

"You're safe noW—"

The rest of Lin's Words Were droWned out by the roar of a motorcycle. He scanned the parking lot and spotted the bike thundering toWard the exit.

TWo patrol cars blocked the opening, but he raised his glove and tWin blasts of fire streaked ahead of him, bloWing the vehicles out of his Way. The rumble of the motorcycle quickly faded

An EMT arrived and Lin handed the burned girl over to him With a final pat on her unburned shoulder.

"We have to get after him," Lin said. "This is too good an opportunity to let him slip through our fingers."

"Don't Worry." Terra joined him near the burned nurse. "That gauntlet is putting out enough magical energy that I'll have no trouble tracking him. I'll call Clair. We're going to need all the help We can get."

* * *

What a fucking rush! Iron Skull roared down the street, his gauntlet still hot and glowing from all the fire he hurled He hadn't had that much fun in years At least until the wizard showed up She made the fire do what she wanted instead of what he wanted He hated her more for that than for spoiling his fun He revved the engine and put on more speed The people on the sidewalk stared at him and Skull gave them a one-finger salute

He glanced over his shoulder No cops Too bad, Skull would have liked to blow up a few more of their cheap-ass cars Despite the lack of pursuit, Skull knew he wasn't in the clear yet Mistress Raven had taught him enough about magic to know that the wizard from the hospital would have no trouble tracking him

Well fuck her and the cops Let 'em come The boys had been itching for a fight since they got to the city last month Today they were going to get it Lucky they had plenty of treats stored up for just such an occasion He turned down a side street toward the rough part of town where his gang had set up shop in an empty flophouse Empty now anyway They'd had to gut a handful of bums and pushers when they first arrived, but the locals quickly learned The Black Skulls were no one they wanted to fuck with

Bloody Skull was standing watch on the front steps of the boarded-up two-story shack when Iron Skull parked in front of the building He had his trademark blood-red bandana tied around his face and the grip of an automatic pistol poked out of the waistband of his oil-stained jeans "All finished, boss?"

Iron Skull ignored the question "Get the boys ready We're going to have company soon "

"What kind of company?"

"The heavily armed, blue kind. Go on."

Bloody Skull let out a war whoop and ran inside. Of all the gang Bloody was the only one that liked to fight more than Iron Skull. He'd get his fill today, no doubt.

Iron Skull drove around to the rear of the flophouse. Across the street was an empty garage beside a collapsed house. He pulled his bike inside next to the others. To keep the guys busy while they waited for Mistress Raven's orders Iron Skull had them dig a tunnel connecting the basement of the flophouse to the garage. His mistress had been kind enough to use her magic to reinforce the tunnel for them so he wasn't worried about it collapsing during the fight with the cops.

Iron Skull switched his bike off and closed the garage door as far as it would go. Hopefully the cops wouldn't notice the bikes parked inside. He crossed the street and Grim opened the door for him. "We really gonna fight the cops, boss?"

Grim sounded like a five-year-old on Christmas morning, or as much like one as a six-and-a-half-foot-tall, three-hundred-and-fifty-pound bald man covered in tattoos could.

"Damn right. I want you upstairs on The Pig. How many ammo belts we got for it?"

"Ten, I think. That's five thousand rounds, right?" Grim wasn't quite as good at math as a five-year-old.

Iron Skull patted his leather-clad shoulder. "Close enough, Grim. Take Tough and a box of grenades with you."

Grim smiled, revealing his three remaining teeth, and ran off to find Tough and the grenades.

Iron Skull went deeper into the house, ignoring the exposed framing and the stink of beer and piss. They'd stayed in worse places over the years. Not much worse, but a little.

"Boss." Bone Skull emerged from a side door. He was dressed in all black, his long hair slicked back from his face and only one tattoo visible. Bone was the only member of the gang that, if he walked down the street, wouldn't draw a second look. That made him useful, but his brain made him Iron Skull's second in command. On the bed behind him, Iron Skull caught a glimpse of machine guns and boxes of ammunition. "What kind of opposition we looking at?"

"Every cop they can call in and at least one wizard. She's good with fire magic so my glove won't be much use until we take her out."

"Easier said than done. Wizards are tricky to deal with, especially surrounded by cops "

Iron Skull nodded. "We'll just have to hope we get lucky and a stray bullet blows her brains out."

"And if we don't get lucky?"

Iron Skull lowered his voice. "That's what the escape tunnel's for. You and me'll split while the others hold them off. You know once they get started the others will never run."

"Bloody won't, that's for sure."

Overhead, Grim stomped around, getting his machine gun set up. It wouldn't be easy for Grim and Tough to make their way downstairs once the bullets started flying. Iron Skull blew out a snort. Who was he kidding? Once the fighting started it would be a wonder if he could pull himself away from the battle. He never felt more alive than when he was an inch from death.

* * *

Lin led a parade of cop cars and two heavily armored SWAT vehicles down the street. Speakers broadcast a warning to the people staring at the passing motorcade to stay inside and aWay from WindoWs until the police gave the all clear.

In the seat beside him Terra stared straight ahead, the magical glasses perched on her nose. She'd been guiding them since they left the hospital ten minutes ago The second Department Wizard, Clair, sat on the back seat muttering in a deep, guttural language. Terra had said Clair Was skilled in earth magic so that Was probably the language she spoke. What the Wizard hoped to accomplish he had no idea. The police Wizard Was busy With a surveillance job and according to the captain couldn't join them.

"Turn left at the next intersection," Terra said. "We're getting close "

A quick look at the neighborhood Would have told Lin that even Without Terra's Warning. He hadn't expected the gang to set up shop in the money district so it Was no surprise they'd moved into the roughest part of the city. It made the tenement they'd visited the other day look positively gentrified. This neighborhood Would have looked right at home in a southern border toWn. The only thing missing Was a pack of half-human heart hunters

"Right there." Terra pointed at a tWo-story house that Was still standing only by a miracle of physics

The roar of a machine gun filled the street. Lin flinched When bullets clattered off the WindShield Without penetrating. The armored trucks raced ahead, draWing fire and forming a barricade in front of the house. Men and Women in body armor carrying machine guns piled out and returned fire.

Something came flying out of the second-story window.

"Grenade!" a SWAT officer shouted.

It exploded just short of the armored vehicle. Shrapnel clattered off the thick steel.

More bullets bounced off the windshield of Lin's car as he maneuvered into the barricade. He slammed it into park as another fusillade of bullets tore through the air Lin reached for the door handle, but Terra laid a restraining hand on his shoulder.

"Stay in here. Bullets can't penetrate the car."

"Why not?"

Terra nodded toward Clair who was still chanting in the strange language. "She's created a barrier that stops anything made of earth from passing through. Since the bullets are lead..."

"And the grenades?" Lin asked.

"It'll stop the shrapnel, but if one goes off too close it might cause the gas tank to explode."

"Terrific. What now?"

"Depends. Do you want prisoners or do you just want me to stop them as fast as I can?"

Lin shook his head at the bizarre situation he found himself in. There was a firefight going on just feet away. Bullets were clattering off his car like raindrops. Yet here he was having a calm conversation just like nothing was happening.

Another grenade went off on the other side of the SWAT van

"A quick decision would be good," Terra said.

"I'm a cop." Lin grasped the steering wheel until his knuckles turned white. "I arrest people. I don't kill them unless I absolutely have to "

Terra looked out the Windshield and raised an eyebroW. "You don't think this falls into the latter category?"

What could he say to that? It looked and sounded like a War out there. He should knoW, he'd fought in one. "Do What you have to "

Terra nodded, her lips set in a grim line She began to chant in What he noW recognized as the language of fire. The Words picked up pace and her tone greW louder.

The roof of the flophouse burst into flame. An explosion from the second floor sent a body flying out the WindoW. It landed in the dirt that passed for a front laWn and didn't move.

A second man stood in the noW-missing WindoW. SWAT concentrated their fire and he fell beside his companion, riddled With dozens of bullets.

Through it all Terra never stopped her spell. The flames spread from the second floor to the first. Smoke billoWed out the WindoWs. The stream of bullets had sloWed to a trickle.

The front door slammed open and a man With a red bandana covering his face stumbled out, firing a pair of submachine guns. A dozen rifles spoke as one and he Went doWn in a heap.

"Where's the guy from the hospital?" Lin asked.

Terra stopped her spell. "He's still in there. His gauntlet is holding back my flames. I'm not sure if he's alone or not."

"I'll tell the SWAT team. We're going to have to dig him out "

"No! Tell them to keep their distance. He may be able to stop the flames, but in about a minute that house is going to collapse. We can dig his body out of the rubble."

* * *

Lady Raven smiled as she watched her minions in the makeshift viewing mirror. One by one they fell to the police and her former comrades at the Department of Magic. It hardly seemed fair, two wizards supported by a small army of cops taking on five bikers with a flame gauntlet. It was a shame. The Black Skulls had been useful pawns, but they'd played their part and like all pawns, there came a time when a sacrifice was necessary. They were loose ends and they needed to be snipped.

It was an interesting, voyeuristic experience, listening to her servants' thoughts as they came to realize they had no hope of winning. Lady Raven had always been closely attuned to dark magic and she fed on despair and negative emotions She focused her will on Iron Skull and settled in to watch the show.

Iron Skull coughed and raised his gauntlet. He'd stopped the flames from reaching them, but not the smoke. The silence from upstairs announced the deaths of Grim and Tough Beside him Bone had his sleeve over his face, trying to filter the fumes. By the front door Bloody was still blasting away between coughs.

The rafters crunched above them. "We gotta go, boss," Bone said.

Iron Skull hated running, but he couldn't deny his lieutenant's grasp of the situation. "Bloody! Time to go."

"Fuck that! I'm not running from these pigs." Bloody roared and charged out the door, a gun in each hand.

The roar of gunfire quickly went silent. So much for Bloody. Iron Skull headed for the little closet that disguised their escape tunnel. He ripped the door off and threw it aside.

His concentration faltered and the flames rushed closer. Iron Skull snarled and mentally commanded them to retreat.

The fire obeyed, but like a hungry lion swirled around at the edge of his control, eager to devour him at a moment's notice.

"Go, Bone. I'm right behind you."

That surprised Lady Raven. She'd figured Iron Skull would toss his man aside to get through the tunnel first. You found loyalty in the oddest places. Shame she hadn't had more time to discover Iron Skull's hidden depths.

The house shook and rumbled as a portion of the roof collapsed. Bone disappeared down the tunnel and Iron Skull leapt in behind him. The dirt walls still looked solid. Ahead of him Bone belly-crawled like mad toward the bikes.

A tremor ran through the walls and dirt clattered off Iron Skull's head. His breathing sped up as he tried to reach Bone. He needed to stay calm. Mistress Raven's magic wouldn't fail them.

Lady Raven laughed out loud at Iron Skull's faith in her magic. If the biker had any idea what she planned he would have taken his chances with the police. Of course, Lady Raven knew he wouldn't. Psychopaths like Iron Skull weren't capable of giving up as long as they thought they had another option. That's why she'd agreed to help them with their stupid tunnel. It was an insurance policy.

One of the police outside knocked on the cheap motel door. "Everything okay, ma'am?"

Her guards must have heard her laughing. "Yeah, just watching a movie. Thanks."

Bone had almost reached the exit when Lady Raven returned her attention to the image in the mirror. She spoke a single harsh word in Infernal, canceling the earth magic she'd used to reinforce the tunnel. It shuddered and collapsed, crushing her pawns and burying them all in one go. The police should thank her for sparing them the trouble of a funeral. Another short spell severed her link with the bikers and caused the small hidden tattoos on their necks to vanish, eliminating any trace of their connection to her. If all went according to plan the investigation should come to a dead end, freeing her to move on with the next phase of the plan.

* * *

The flophouse collapsed with a resounding crash. The moment it did Terra spoke a short phrase and the fire extinguished and the embers cooled. Behind her Clair fell silent. The fight had been fierce, but short. They had the bikers outnumbered and overwhelmed in terms of both magic and weapons. The confrontation ended the only way possible. It all seemed like such a waste. What had the thugs hoped to accomplish?

Lin climbed out and Terra and Clair joined him. He looked over his car and shook his head. "Not a scratch on it."

Clair raised an eyebrow. "You sound disappointed."

"Maybe a little. A few bullet holes would have been a good excuse to ask for a new car. This one's on its last legs."

"I'll remember that the next time we're in a firefight," Clair said

"I'm not complaining." Lin waved his hands.

"Hey, Lin?" One of the SWAT team members jogged over. Judging from the bars on his arm he was the team commander. "If you feel the scene's secure my guys are ready to go."

Lin glanced at Terra She closed her eyes and cast a simple light magic spell. There was nothing living in the rubble. "We're good. It's a recovery mission now."

"You heard the lady." Lin and the SWAT leader shook hands. "Thanks, John. You're the best."

John jumped into the back of the SWAT van and a moment later they rolled out. The side of the van was pocked with bullet holes and slashed from shrapnel, but none of it had gone through to the interior. They really built those things tough. Terra slipped her glasses on and found a faint magical aura around both vans. Magical reinforcement helped too.

"Are you two going to hang around?" Lin asked. "Cleaning this mess'll take a while. We'll need to bring the bomb squad down along with some heavy equipment."

"I need to find the fire gauntlet and whatever they had hidden in that niche at the cafe. Until those items are secured a wizard needs to be on the scene."

"I'll head back to the office and inform Chief Kane," Clair said.

Terra nodded and Lin said, "I'll get an officer to take you."

While Lin got one of the uniformed officers to take Clair back to the office, Terra walked over to the collapsed building and muttered, "Reveal."

When nothing immediately popped out at her she slipped the glasses on to magnify the energy. There was a very weak lingering dark aura that matched the energy from the cafe. Those coffers must have been here either before or after they were taken to the hidden storage niche.

She also picked up a stronger fire aura, but not as strong as she would have expected if the gauntlet was buried under the rubble. Terra traced it to the edge of the ruined house where it vanished. Frowning, she walked all the way around the perimeter of the house and found no energy signature strong enough to be the gauntlet. Even under the rubble it should have glowed like a light bulb to her magical senses

Terra returned to the last place she saw the magical energy. She stood facing the street. It was headed that way when it vanished. Did the biker from the hospital have some sort of suppressing container? There was no way to know without digging down to the body. She'd just have to be patient.

Lin joined her as the patrolmen began setting a perimeter with yellow tape. "I called in the cleanup crews. It'll take days to sift the rubble and deal with any unexploded ordinance. I don't suppose there's any magic that could speed the process along?"

"Despite what some of the more arrogant wizards like to pretend, there are limits to what magic can do. I'm afraid you'll have to sort this out the mundane way. I'd appreciate it if you started right there " She pointed at the last place she sensed the gauntlet.

"Considering everything you've done for us since this investigation began I think we can accommodate your request." Lin grinned. "After all, we have to start somewhere."

Chapter 7

Party Crashers

"The wizards killed Mort, just like Black Bird said they would." Michael paced in the close quarters of the tiny apartment that served as the official church of the True Face of God The four other members of his congregation watched his agitated movements with bright, eager eyes. They knew, as he knew, that the time for their glorious retribution was nigh. "For that heinous act God will punish them. He will punish them through our hands"

"Amen!" Gabriel raised his hands in praise. Brother Gabriel was always the most demonstrative of his little congregation. He'd lost his job as a demolition worker when the company switched to using magical constructs to pull down derelict buildings. For safety, they claimed, but everyone knew the truth. The wizards had enchanted the weak-willed suits into doing what they wanted.

"Though he wasn't a member of our congregation, Brother Call was still a fellow traveler on the true path. As a sign of our faith and to honor our fallen brother we will finish the good work he started We will kill the boy wizard before his powers can be unlocked and his soul condemned to Hell for all eternity. Though it may cost him his life we can still save him from damnation It's our duty "

That brought smiles to the faces of men eager to do God's work These were good men, strong both in body and in faith They couldn't fail, especially since Black Bird told them everything they needed to know, both when and how to best accomplish their noble mission

"Brother John " Michael focused his intense gaze on the youngest member of their group, a man of only nineteen years who'd been denied his rightful place at college due to the foul influences of magic "Did you bring the item?"

John reached into the pocket of his ragged army surplus jacket and pulled out a small device with a screen and several buttons Michael wasn't a technical person, his skills lay in a more divine direction, but Brother John worked at an electronics store and had a gift for cobbling together technology

"Are you sure this is right? I felt bad about stealing the components from my boss "

Michael bent down and stared into John's watery brown eyes "We're doing God's work, son There can be no crime while we're acting in his name Will it work?"

"Yes, sir I tested it with my phone and it blocked the signal from several hundred yards and weakened it for a third of a mile "

Michael clapped the youth on his bony shoulder "Good man I knew I could count on you "

John puffed up at the compliment and sat up straighter. He'd do what was necessary. Michael saw it in his eyes.

"Brother Jacob." Michael turned to the oldest member of the group, a still-spry sixty-year-old who ran a pawn shop and found the True Face of God after surviving a brush with cancer. "Did you bring the weapons?"

"Sure did, though a stranger collection of gear I never seen." Jacob unzipped a green duffle bag and laid the weapons on Michael's battered coffee table. First came a baseball bat, then a pair of chef's knives, a three-pound sledgehammer, and last a wrecking bar. "How come we can't just take guns? I have plenty of them at the shop "

"The wizard's vile magic protects the building. Black Bird says only weapons that are also tools can pass through." Michael made the sign of the cross and spoke a prayer in Latin. "With God's blessing these humble implements will see his task complete "

Ezra snatched up the baseball bat. Heavyset and balding, Ezra had seen some rough years before he found his way to Michael and the church. He caressed the grip of the bat. "I was the star shortstop in high school Feels good to hold a bat again "

Michael smiled and folded his hands together. "It will feel even better when you use it to send the heathen to meet his maker. Take up your weapons, brothers. We go to do God's work."

The congregation left Michael's apartment and piled into his white panel van. He settled in behind the wheel and turned the key. The starter whined and refused to catch. He paused and looked to heaven. "Dear Lord, if you wish us to complete your divine work please make this useless pile of metal start up."

He tried the key again and with a little divine intervention the motor sputtered to life The guys gave a round of Hallelujahs and Michael pulled out They drove through the streets, watching the people go about their business, indifferent to the blasphemies surrounding them That would all change tonight when they announced the abomination's death on the evening news

Fifteen minutes later they parked in the garage under the wizard's building There were only a few cars at this time of day so they had no trouble getting a spot close to the elevator Though Michael had no intention of retreating it always paid to be careful

"Are you sure we should be doing this in the middle of the day?" John asked

"Of course " Michael raised his fist "We will bring judgment in the bright light of day "

"Besides," Jacob said "Everybody's at work right now Fewer people to call the police before we finish our work "

"That too " Michael slammed the transmission into park and they climbed out of the van "Brother John, up to the roof Call us when you're in position and you're ready to activate the device "

"Yes, Michael " The young man scurried into the elevator and pressed the button for the roof

When he'd gone Ezra said, "Shame the kid's going to miss the important work "

"John has a gentle soul " Michael pulled his knife and tested the edge "He would be a liability to us in a fight "

"Ain't going to be no fight " Gabriel slapped the wrecking bar into the palm of his hand making a meaty smack "It's going to be a slaughter "

* * *

Conryu closed the big book of boring magic and banged his head on the cover. He'd been reading at the dining room table in an effort to keep from falling asleep. It had been a Week since he began his house arrest and Conryu finally finished the stupid book.

Much as he might complain, if you looked past the mystic mumbo jumbo it appeared magic Was nothing more than a system of energy manipulation that you altered to create the effects you Wanted. As long as he looked at it that Way he found he could Wrap his head around it pretty Well. The problem Was Whoever Wrote the book liked to couch everything in supernatural terms instead of just saying straight out What she meant.

The alarm on his phone rang and Conryu glanced at the clock. Eleven exactly. Jonny and Rin Were supposed to have lunch With him and Maria. Mrs. Kane had gone out of toWn for a job so they Were all going to Watch the opening match of the Four Nations Magical Tournament together in Conryu's apartment. It Wasn't like he could go anyWhere.

Maria didn't think much of the North American team this year. Conryu had no idea if the team Was any good, all he kneW Was this Was Heather James's last year and the blond team captain Was one of the hottest Women he'd ever seen. He'd have to be careful not to drool or Maria Would give him a smack.

Conryu collected the bag of chips and fresh salsa his mom had picked up for him and spread them out on the living room table. The others Were supposed to bring sandWich fixings and more snacks. Five minutes later his doorbell rang. Maria Was Waiting on the other side With rolls and deli meat. "I'm the first to arrive?"

He grinned. "Yup, though you had the shortest trip. I finally finished the stupid book."

"But did you understand it?" Maria slipped inside.

"I think I understand the principles, how the various types of energy interact, that sort of thing. What I can't figure out is why people who wield certain types of energy wouldn't get along."

"It's not that the people don't get along, it's that the energy doesn't combine well with its direct opposite." Maria put the meat in the fridge and the rolls on the counter "Some wizards also have a tendency to get mixed up in the politics of elemental spirits which can lead to arguments as well. Those who specialize in one type of magic tend to view the world through the lens of that magical philosophy and it colors everything else It's stupid on a lot of levels, but then wizards aren't so different than any other group of people "

Conryu sighed, still not really getting it. "It sounds sort of like the arguments Harley guys and Indian guys have."

"That's as good an analogy as any. When are the others supposed to arrive?"

"Any time now." Someone knocked. "Speak of the devil."

Conryu was surprised Jonny arrived first. He figured if anyone would arrive early it would be Rin. Jonny had a cooler with him, hopefully stocked with soda. "Hey, bro. Did I miss anything?"

"Nope, we've got ten minutes before the start. What'd you bring?"

"Root beer, cola, and mineral water for the ladies."

"Bless your heart, Jonny Salazar," Maria said in an over-the-top southern accent

The boys shared a laugh at that. Maria's phone rang and while she talked Conryu and Jonny broke into the chips and salsa. A few seconds later Maria joined them on the couch.

"Who was it?" Conryu asked.

"Rin. She can't make it, her little brother's sitter had to go home early. It's weird, my phone cut off in the middle of our conVersation."

Conryu shrugged. That happened now and then. No big deal. Since Rin wasn't coming they fixed themselves some sandwiches and settled in.

The announcer came on the tV. "Ladies and gentlemen, welcome to the 567th annual Four Nations Tournament. This year's odds-on faVorite is the Empire of the Rising Sun's team with four seniors and two juniors returning to compete."

"Who do you like?" Maria asked.

"Heather James," Conryu and Jonny answered together.

He thought maybe that wasn't the wisest answer an instant before she smacked him on the back of the head. The blow didn't surprise him in the least, but it still stung. "I meant which team. All the guys and many of the girls like Heather James. I read online she's got a modeling contract waiting for her after she graduates."

That surprised Conryu less than the slap. "I don't know. If the Alliance doesn't haVe a chance I guess I should root for the Empire, since that's where Dad comes from."

"Yeah, that's who I'm going for," Maria said.

"I've got twenty bucks on the Kingdom," Jonny said.

The camera shifted to the arena floor and they stopped talking. There were no seats since the people monitoring the event didn't allow a live audience on the off chance a spell went out of control Outside the arena dozens of lounges had been built with large-screen tvs, bars and restaurants for the patrons, and plenty of gambling halls

The tournament was being held in the Republic of Australia this year, though no one gave their team much chance of success A group of girls stood at each of the cardinal directions They wore robes associated with their element and school patches on the back

"What are they starting with this year?" Conryu asked

"Group casting It's the trickiest discipline and requires the most teamwork " Maria took a bite of her sandwich

That was one of the last chapters Conryu had read and he hadn't fully understood it Something about layering spells so opposing energies didn't come into contact

The Empire team and Australian team moved to the edge of the arena leaving the Alliance to face off with the Kingdom of the Isles team in the first match Five members of the Alliance team raised their hands Heather took the lead, chanting a spell, her blue-green robe swirling around her, outlining the exquisite figure underneath as the power built She was stunning, like someone out of a story

"Oh man," Jonny groaned

Maria glared at him then shifted her gaze to Conryu He kept his expression neutral, barely

A water dragon appeared above her Next it was wrapped in a skin of swirling energy by the wind mage, followed by scales of fire and spikes of earth Last the light mage cast a spell, but nothing happened

"Did her magic not work?" Conryu asked.

"It worked," Maria said. "Light magic can interact with all four elements She used her spell to bind the construct into a complete whole. The results aren't visible, but they're probably the most important if the team wants to win."

"What now?"

"Just watch," Maria said.

A single member of the Kingdom team stepped forward. She wore a black robe and carried a rod tipped with some sort of round black gem. She chanted in a language both guttural and entrancing. Conryu had never heard anything like it. Those strange words spoke to him, called him. He leaned closer, his food forgotten

Beside him Maria shivered and set her snack down. On the screen, power gathered around the gem, throwing off black sparks. The chant built to a crescendo. With the final word the wizard in black thrust the rod at the dragon construct.

An orb of dark energy streaked toward the dragon. It clashed into the stone spikes, smashed through the fire scales, shredded the wind skin and exposed inside the watery center, blowing the construct to shards of energy.

"Told you they were going to lose." Maria hugged herself and tried to act like nothing had happened.

For his part Conryu couldn't get those words out of his mind. He wanted to hear more.

The match went to commercial and a few seconds later someone knocked. "I thought you said Rin wasn't coming?"

"That's what she told me. Maybe something happened."

Conryu shrugged and walked to the door He looked through the peephole and saw the familiar mass of white hair He groaned and opened the door "Can't you take a hint?"

"Sorry, my boy," the professor said "I just thought you might li—"

"Die, abomination!"

Conryu looked down the hall Four men carrying an assortment of improvised weapons roared out of the elevator and charged

Conryu grabbed the professor and yanked him inside before bolting the door "We've got company!"

* * *

Lady Raven booted up her laptop and logged in to the secure forum using a proxy server After a few days the tiny motel room had grown confining It would be a relief when the police finally completed their work and let her go

She'd sent the zealots all the information they needed to infiltrate the building and kill the boy the day before yesterday It hadn't been difficult to determine when Shizuku Kane would be out of the city and the rest was simply understanding how the building's wards functioned—child's play for a wizard of her skill

The question was did the cultists have the courage of their convictions, or were they nothing but talk? Hopefully the death of their compatriot would properly motivate them If that didn't do it she didn't know what would

There was a single private message waiting for Black Bird She smiled and clicked on it The cultists were attacking today a little before noon She checked the time Quarter after eleven She had to hurry

She tossed the laptop on the bed and stood up The only mirror in her piddling little room Was in the bathroom. Not ideal, but it Would Work. She stepped into the cramped bathroom and locked the door behind her. She doubted the cops outside Would barge in on her, but Why risk it?

A Wind spell linked the mirror to a minor spirit and sent it soaring out over the city. What it saW appeared on the mirror. After a number of scouting runs she kneW exactly Where Conryu's building lay and hoW to get there. Her Will guided the spirit and soon the roof of the building came into vieW. A young man stood there With a small device in his hand. That had to be the cell scrambler she told them to bring

Excellent, the attack Was either already underWay or soon Would be. She commanded the spirit to remain in place and chanted another spell Though Lady Raven preferred to use shadoW beasts for jobs like this, the bright daylight rendered that Impossible

Fortunately, sunlight didn't bother actual demons in the least and she kneW the true names of tWo that Would like nothing better than to have a chance to rend the flesh from a foolish mortal. Not that the other demons she'd dealt With over the years didn't enjoy a bit of rending. It seemed to be one of the prime pastimes in Hell

With the Wind spirit serving as a focus Lady Raven opened a small portal above the building and called the names of her hunters. The black-Winged demons hurtled through the gate, eager to ansWer her call.

They plummeted toWard the cultist on the roof. Their bloodlust Washed over her through the spell that connected them. Her face flushed and her fingers curled like claws. Nothing would have pleased her more in that moment than to feel the man's blood oozing through her talons.

She clenched her fists. "No."

Lady Raven refused to let the demons overwhelm her.

The hunters continued their descent. They'd reach the cultist in moments. If they damaged the signal disrupter her true prey might call for help

"No!"

The demons pulled up short and soared away. Their rage at being denied prey flooded through the link. She forced the feelings away. The demons obeyed her, not the other way around. If she didn't maintain control of herself and of them it would lead to a bloodbath. No bad thing in and of itself, but not what she desired at the moment

She formed an image of Conryu in her mind and thrust it into the demons' brains through their link, along with an unspoken threat that if they let him escape it would be the end of them. The hunters shrieked their anger to the heavens, but it did nothing to affect her will.

She commanded They obeyed Period

* * *

"Dude, what's going on?"

A heavy blow struck the door before he could answer Jonny's question. A second blow struck and the tip of a crowbar appeared through the wood.

"That door won't hold them long." Conryu turned to the trembling professor. "Do you know those guys?"

"We rode up on the elevator together. I didn't notice the weapons."

Another crash rattled the door.

Jonny and Maria Were both on their feet and looking more than a little Worried. Conryu didn't blame them. HoW many times did someone have to try and kill you before it became routine?

Maria Whipped her phone out and dialed. She shook her head "No signal "

"Try the landline. Jonny, help me push the couch against the door "

The boys ran behind the couch and shoved it until the far end hit the door frame

"No dial tone!" Maria slammed the receiver back doWn.

"What should I do?" the professor asked.

"Stay out of the Way." Conryu brushed past him and Went to Maria. "I didn't think you could bring Weapons into this building "

"You can't."

A resounding crash blasted one of the panels out of the door

"Really?"

A face appeared in the opening. It Was a man in his late thirties With a full beard and Wild, crazy eyes. "Give us the abomination and the rest of you Will be spared."

"Eat shit!" Jonny shouted.

The man snarled and WithdreW. A moment later the pounding resumed

"We've got a minute, maybe tWo." Conryu looked around, but the only Weapons Were kitchen knives. Hardly ideal. "We'll have to take the fire escape."

"You're not supposed to leave the building," Maria said.

"Inside's looking as lot less safe than it did yesterday." Conryu led the way to his parents' bedroom where the fire escape attached to the building

Maria dragged on his arm. "The wizard might have sent them in to flush you out. Who knows what kind of monster might be waiting outside."

Conryu went straight to the window and pulled it open. "I'll take my chances with potential monsters over sure-thing murderers." He motioned her through, then the professor and Jonny. Conryu climbed out last and slammed the window shut. It wouldn't even slow a crowbar, but maybe one of those assholes would cut himself.

A hideous shriek was followed by a...something, slamming into an invisible wall inches from the railing. It had black wings like a crow; long, thin limbs that ended in curved talons; and a fang-filled mouth that took up half its face.

Jonny scrambled away from the creature and pressed his back against the building. "What the hell is that?"

"A demon!" Maria and the professor shouted.

A second creature almost identical to the first slammed into the barrier. Three-inch claws scrabbled against thin air as it tried to reach them. Maria shot him her patented I told you so look.

"Up or down?" Conryu shouted over the screams of the demons

"Down," Maria answered without a moment's thought.

"Go, Jonny. I'll bring up the rear."

192

Conryu didn't have to tell his friend twice. Jonny's sneakers clanged on the metal steps as he ran down them. The professor followed at a slower, but still hurried pace. Maria looked back at him, her eyes wide. He squeezed her shoulder and gave her a little nudge toward the steps.

She'd barely moved when the sledgehammer crashed through the window, missing Conryu by inches. He snapped a kick that caught the guy's wrist as it swung past. He didn't connect cleanly, but he knocked the attacker off balance so he fell halfway out the window and lost his grip on his weapon.

When hands grabbed the attacker's belt to help pull him out of the way Conryu ran for it. Maria had cleared the first landing, giving him a clear path. He bounded down the steps four at a time, catching up with the others in seconds.

"What do we do when we hit the ground?" Conryu asked when he reached Maria. A few feet away the demons soared back and forth, just waiting for them to leave the protection of Mrs. Kane's wards.

"Hug the wall. It looks like Mom's wards extend about three feet from the wall. As long as we stay in that safe zone the demons can't reach us."

"You hear that, Jonny?"

"Loud and clear, bro "

Conryu started to ask the professor, but the old man was busy gagging and tossing his lunch over the railing The demons lunged for him, but Conryu managed to jerk him back to safety.

"Careful. You don't want to die before you can prove your theory, do you?"

The professor coughed and wiped his mouth "I'm not used to this much exercise Even in my youth I preferred the vicarious thrills of a good book "

The heavy tread of boots on metal announced the pending arrival of their unwelcome guests

"Suck it up, Professor We need to move " Conryu gave him a gentle shove towards Jonny who'd stopped and looked back "Keep him moving "

Jonny nodded and grabbed Angus by the wrist, half encouraging and half dragging him along Conryu and Maria followed as closely as they dared

Conryu glanced up There were only two guys behind them The others must have gone around to cut them off Only three more floors and they'd reach the pavement Should he stand and fight when their numbers were divided? It would be tricky fighting armed men given the space limitations

They reached the final landing and Conryu still didn't know what to do "Any thoughts?"

"We just need to hold out a little while longer," Maria said "Mom would have sensed it the moment those demons struck her barrier She'll call Dad and he'll send help "

"How long?"

She shook her head "Maybe ten minutes "

"Shit!" Ten minutes surrounded by demons and lunatics might as well be ten hours

Ahead of them Jonny had the professor smushed up flat against the wall "Dude, which way?"

Behind them a broad-shouldered guy in his thirties carrying a crowbar started down the ladder to the ground The nut with the sledgehammer stood on the platform above. Conryu stepped back, set himself, and lashed out with a side kick that struck between the ladder rungs.

The force of the blow sent Crowbar Man flying out into the alley between his building and the one next door. He landed with a dull thud. When the demons didn't immediately fly down and rip him to pieces it confirmed what Maria had guessed. The killers and the demons were working together.

"Head for the garage," Maria said. "At least we'll be safe from the demons"

* * *

At least they'll be safe from the demons. For some reason, as they ran through the almost-empty garage, that thought kept running through Conryu's head. He had the professor by one arm, Jonny had the other and between them they almost carried him. It would be hours before anyone returned home from work. Ninety percent of the residents worked for the government and came and went on the same schedule as his mother.

The professor stumbled and fell to the concrete. "I can't take another step." He held his head between his knees and gasped for breath

Conryu looked around, but there was nowhere to hide. They'd intentionally run away from the elevator on the assumption that the other killers would be around there somewhere. They'd gotten a small lead on the two that followed them down the fire escape and lost them when they ducked into the garage

He'd explored the building with Maria when they were kids, but his brain had frozen. There had to be somewhere to hide until the cavalry arrived He shot Maria a pleading look She shook her head

"What now, dude?"

Why did Jonny keep asking that? Conryu had no idea what to do next Running for their lives was the best he could come up with upstairs and he hadn't thought up anything better yet Unfortunately the professor was blown and running was no longer an option, unless they were willing to leave the helpless old man to the tender mercies of a group of deranged killers Conryu didn't especially like the professor, but he couldn't leave him to die

"Conryu " Maria's voice held a hint of hope and when he looked where she pointed he grinned

"I love you, you know that?"

He'd completely overlooked the fire hose hanging behind a glass door on the wall That thing shot water with enough force to strip the paint off a car He'd seen it used when a rusty, piece of crap hatchback had caught fire his junior year

Conryu crouched down in front of the professor "Climb aboard "

With Jonny's help he maneuvered the professor onto his back and carried him piggyback out of the way He lowered Angus to the ground and leaned him against the wall Maria crouched beside him and nodded that she'd look after him

Jonny smashed the glass out and yanked the hose free The tread of heavy boots and shouts echoing through the garage hastened them along

"You want to aim or work the valve?" Conryu asked

"Aim I owe these bitches a bath "

Conryu grinned and handed his friend the brass nozzle. They bumped fists and Conryu Went back to the round valve. He gave the valve a test tWist and found it free and ready to go.

And not a moment too soon. All four guys rounded the corner, spotted them, and charged

Conryu spun the valve all the Way open and a moment later a gusher blasted out, hitting the nearest man in the chest and sending him spraWling. Jonny Wrestled the poWerful floW into the big guy With the hammer, knocking him to the ground as Well.

The bucking hose Was giving Jonny all he could handle so Conryu grabbed it a feW feet behind his friend to stabilize his aim. BetWeen the tWo of them they Washed the killers doWn the garage until they Were out of range.

The four men scrambled to their feet and looked intent on charging straight Into the stream a second time Conryu hoped they Were that stupid.

One of them Wasn't. The man With the beard that Wanted Conryu to turn himself over grabbed the others and held them back. He pulled out a Walkie-talkie and spoke into it. Conryu tensed, ready for Whatever they planned next. And Where Was the backup Maria had assured him Would be on the Way?

What he Wasn't ready for Was the Water floW to come to a sudden stop. He glanced back, but the mechanism looked fine. Something must have happened someWhere else. Conryu had no idea Where the main shutoff Was, but apparently someone had found It

The bearded man brandished a chef's knife and the killers stalked forWard. "No more of your tricks, monster.

God has decreed that you must die, just like every magic using abomination in this corrupt world If you don't resist I promise you a quick end."

Conryu bared his teeth If this prick thought he'd just stand by and let his throat be cut he didn't know who he was talking to "Let go of the nozzle and move back I need some room," he whispered

Jonny looked at the heavy brass nozzle then back at Conryu with a knowing smile "Fuck 'em up" He moved back beside Maria and the professor, giving Conryu a good fifteen feet of clear space, plenty for what he had planned

Apparently the boss killer misunderstood "Your friend has abandoned you, just as God has You are alone in the world Kill him."

A middle-aged man with a baseball bat sauntered toward him, looking far more confident than he had any right to Conryu waited until he was about twenty feet away then he set the hose to spinning He built up momentum until the killer closed to within ten feet then he let it fly

The brass nozzle hit the idiot square in the face with the force of a cannonball Teeth and blood flew everywhere His nose crushed flat and the front of his face caved in The bat clattered to the floor followed in short order by the man that had been holding it

Conryu snapped the nozzle back and set it spinning again The three killers still conscious and on their feet shared a considerably less confident look The older man with the crowbar didn't worry Conryu The long chunk of iron looked far too heavy for him to handle in a fight The big guy with the sledgehammer was another matter. He held his weapon easily, like someone with long familiarity.

"Come on, boys," Conryu said. "Say a prayer and step right up. See if God is inclined to turn aside my weapon."

The leader looked at the big guy who looked right back, clearly in no hurry to have his face smashed in. Conryu almost wished they'd charge. He couldn't keep the nozzle spinning forever.

The leader pulled his walkie-talkie out again. Conryu felt pressure building in the hose and had just time enough to toss it aside before it went berserk, spraying water every which way and thrashing like a beheaded snake. Looked like the boss had more brains than Conryu had first thought.

The three killers charged. Conryu did the last thing he figured they'd expect: he ran right toward the big guy with the hammer.

The hammerhead came right at his skull. Conryu slid under the attack. His opponent used too much power and lost his balance. Conryu gave him an uppercut to the groin. He didn't care how big the guy was, that would put him out of commission for a while.

Hammer Man's pained, high-pitched squeal was music to Conryu's ears. Even sweeter was the sound of the sledgehammer hitting the concrete floor.

He snatched up the weapon, whirled, and hurled it at the cultist with the crowbar as hard as he could.

The heavy steel hammerhead crashed into the unfortunate killer's left thigh. His leg bent at an impossible angle as his femur shattered from the impact. Conryu turned his cool regard on the leader. He narrowed his eyes and locked gazes with the man like his father had taught him

Conryu strode forward, ignoring the moans and groans of the injured men. "You're all alone now. Unless you expect God to show up and save you. Me? I wouldn't count on it."

"You won't shake my faith, abomination. Even if I fall here, I do so secure in the knowledge that I served my God until the end." The leader laid the chef's knife along his forearm and beckoned Conryu forward.

Looked like this one knew how to use a blade at least. Conryu took a step.

"Watch out, bro!"

Conryu ducked in time to see Jonny come flying past. The bat he'd picked up from the unconscious killer crashed into the leader's head and sent him to the ground.

Jonny raised the bat for another stroke, but Conryu caught his wrist. "Fight's over. Thanks."

Jonny's breath rasped and the muscles in his jaw bunched. It looked like a huge effort for him to lower the bat. Conryu gently took it out of his hands before he let go of his friend's wrist.

Conryu kicked the knife away from the unconscious leader. The fight was over, he reminded himself. They were safe for the moment. He didn't know about the next moment, but for now Conryu would take what he could get.

Chapter 8

A Parting Clue

L in parked in front of the motel the police department used as a safe house. It Was nothing fancy, just a cheap, tWo-story affair With maybe thirty rooms. While it Wasn't luxury, Lin had made sure the place Was clean and secure. He oWed Lacy that much for her help.

A full day had passed since the most recent attempt on Conryu's life. The bomb techs Were still searching the ruins of the bikers' base and it looked like they'd need several more days before the excavators started to dig. HoW many times Was he going to ansWer a call saying the boy had been attacked, shoW up, and scrape a bunch of idiot cultists off the ground? You'd think if Conryu laid out enough of them the rest Would take a hint and find another target. Of course that Would be rational behavior, not the sort of thing you thought of Where zealots Were involved.

In addition to the continued attacks, Lieutenant Smith of the bomb squad had announced an additional delay to the excavation of the flophouse. When he made that announcement

Lin had feared Terra might turn him into a frog, assuming wizards could actually do that. When she'd calmed down he'd dropped her off at her car with a promise to call as soon as they got the all clear. Apparently unable to leave it alone for two or three days she'd called this morning and asked to take another look around.

Two uniformed officers, a big white guy and a skinny black guy, sat in cheap folding chairs on either side of the door to room 1B. They jumped to their feet the moment they recognized Lin.

He climbed out of his car, flashed his badge more out of habit than necessity, and knocked on the door. A moment later Lacy's purple hair appeared in the gap in the doorway. "Hi, Detective."

She closed the door, undid the safety chain, and opened it all the way. She had a cheap white motel robe tied around her. Poor girl looked exhausted. "Miss Winn, may I came in?"

"Always so polite." She stepped aside. "Welcome to my humble home."

Lin stepped inside and she closed the door behind him. Humble was certainly the word for her room. Single bed, nightstand, cheap tv on a cheaper table. If that bed felt as hard as it looked it was no wonder she had circles under her eyes.

"What brings you by?" Lacy asked.

"I've come to set you free." He reached into his jacket pocket and pulled out a plane ticket. "One way to Central City, as promised. Your information was a huge help. Consider your record clean. If you want to get dressed and pack I can take you to the airport."

She hugged him. "That's awesome, Detective. Just give me fifteen minutes."

He left the room and she shut the door From another pocket Lin removed a folded-over packet of papers. "You guys have been reassigned. Thanks for looking after her."

The officers on duty each accepted a bundle. "Our pleasure, Detective," the black officer said.

"Yeah, though many more days of this and I'd have gone into a coma," the White officer added. "Not that the girl Was any trouble, just the opposite, We hardly heard a peep out of her."

Since Lin had been shot at and nearly roasted to death he Wasn't overly interested in their complaints. "I'm sure the duty officer Will find something more exciting for you to do."

The officers piled into their vehicle and left the parking lot. Lin Watched them until they'd gone out of sight. Maybe he could coax someone into giving him a boring case once he'd tied this one up

Lacy emerged from her room having exchanged her robe for ripped jeans and a tank top. A green army surplus bag dangled from her shoulder. She Was aWfully skinny. Maybe he should offer to stop at a diner on the Way to the airport.

"All set?"

"Yup "

Lin opened the passenger-side door for her She smiled and shook her head before tossing her bag in the back seat and climbing in. Lin joined her and fired up the car. It Was only fifteen minutes to the airport and they had plenty of time before Lacy's flight took off.

"Do you Want to stop for something to eat on the Way?" he asked.

"That's sweet, but I already had something this morning You've been great and all, don't think I don't appreciate that, but I'm ready to blow this town "

Lin smiled "Fair enough Want to hear how we found your bikers? They're all dead so I can tell you "

"Thanks anyway It's all above my pay grade There is one thing I'm curious about Did you ever catch up to my boss? That prick still owes me a week's pay "

"I'm afraid not He probably spotted us at the cafe and took off We have his picture out everywhere It's only a matter of time until we find him "

"Maybe you could rough him up a little for me "

Lin laughed They spent the rest of the ride in amiable silence until he pulled up at the busy main gate Lacy jumped out then reached back for her bag

"Are you meeting someone in the capital?" Lin asked

"I have a sister there I'll call her before my flight takes off Thanks again, Detective "

Lacy shut the car door, waved, and ran toward the terminal Lin blew out a sigh, said a silent prayer that she'd be okay, and drove off to meet Terra at the biker's house

The crosstown journey took half an hour, not including the fifteen minutes he spent at a sandwich shop picking up two BLTs to share with Terra As he drove he found himself wondering if the attractive lady wizard would like to join him for a more formal meal, dinner with a nice bottle of wine maybe

When he arrived the techs were poking the pile of rubble with probes connected to a laptop Terra stood by the curb beside her car, toe tapping and arms crossed Maybe she was hungry Free food always put people in a better mood

He parked behind her and got out, paper bags in one hand and bottles of water in the other. "Morning. Have you been waiting long?"

"No. What's in the bag?"

"Lunch. You hungry?" Lin offered her a bag and bottle.

"Thank you." She opened the bag and smiled. "I love BLTs. How did you know?"

Lin hadn't had a clue, instead acting on the assumption that everyone loved bacon. "I am a detective. What news from the world of magic?"

"Nothing beyond my boss wanting me to recover the artifacts as quickly as possible and track Mercia while I'm at it."

"Any luck?" Lin dug in to his sandwich.

"No on both counts. What about you?"

"I actually had a good morning. I took our witness to the airport." He smiled and shook his head. "I'd never heard someone her age use the expression 'above my pay grade' before."

Terra dropped her sandwich. "Are you certain that's the exact expression she used?"

"Yeah, why?" Lin took a drink to moisten his suddenly dry throat

"Mercia used that same expression all the time. Especially when she was bitter about her position in the Department."

"You don't think...?"

"I do think." Terra dug the now-familiar glasses out of her gray robe and slipped them on. "She rode with you this morning?"

"Yeah, like an hour ago."

Terra marched back to his car, muttering as she went. She stopped beside the passenger-side door and scowled. "There are remnants of illusion magic present on the seat and in the air "

Lin had lost his appetite "Was it Mercia?"

"No way to know for sure, but I'd bet a month's pay it was" Terra slammed her fist on the roof "Damn it all to hell! She was right in front of us and I missed it"

* * *

Lady Raven jogged into the airport, eager to get out of the detective's sight She'd enjoyed the Lacy Winn persona, but her usefulness had ended The cops had been kind enough to deal with all her loose ends and the Skulls had placed the shadow gems where she'd instructed Now the only living person that knew where they'd been hidden was her and she had no intention of telling anyone

Hundreds of people ran from gate to baggage claim through security and to the crappy restaurants None of them had a clue how the world would change and all thanks to her She'd worked for months under the noses of her so-called superiors at the Department of Magic and they had never guessed It would be sweet indeed when they finally learned who had brought about their downfall

Only her failure to deal with Conryu Koda left a bitter taste on her mouth Lady Raven swallowed a curse After the zealots had failed and Shizuku Kane had banished her demons she'd severed the connection between the mirror and the wind spirit Fortunately that attempt hadn't required her to expend any Society resources, just a group of worthless, deluded men and a little of her personal magic She wouldn't be mentioning the little episode to the Hierarchs when she next spoke to them

Yes, it would certainly be wise to keep this most recent failure to herself, especially since they essentially ordered her not to even make the attempt in the first place.

Lady Raven made her way to the help desk. Though she doubted it would do anything to improve her mood she decided to make a petty, almost childish gesture. Even wizards got to act childishly once in a while. "Excuse me."

A middle-aged woman with curly brown hair looked up at her with a flat, bored expression. "Can I help you?"

"Would it be possible for me to leave a message for a friend here? He forgot his ticket."

"Sure." She handed Lady Raven a blank envelope and a pen. "Write it on here and I'll log it into the system. If he checks at any of the stations someone will tell him we have it."

"Thanks so much." She jotted a quick note on the inside of the envelope, wrote "Detective Chang" on the front, and sealed the ticket inside. "I can't thank you enough."

The woman accepted the envelope with a disinterested grunt then set to typing on her terminal Lady Raven left her to it and headed for the ladies' room.

The stall farthest from the door was empty. Inside, she released her youthful illusion and changed into a black dress. A less elaborate spell altered her hair and face enough that no one would recognize her as either Mercia or Lacy. That done Lady Raven headed to the front of the airport where the taxis waited. She'd be long gone before the good detective even considered looking for her, assuming he ever did.

An hour and a half later found her once more standing in a spell circle wearing her raven mask and facing the Hierarchs.

She couldn't judge their emotions behind the masks, but none of them looked angry That was enough for Lady Raven

"I trust you've cleaned up your mess," Lady Tiger said

They didn't seem to know about her most recent failed attempt to kill the boy Thank heaven for that "Yes, I'm now the only living person who knows where the shadow gems are hidden We can activate them whenever you wish "

"You know better," Lady Wolf said "We can't activate them until the floating island returns "

She had in fact only suspected that Despite her efforts in enchanting the gems she hadn't developed the spell, only cast it "What of me? Do the Hierarchs have a task for me in the meantime?"

"You will tend the gems," Lady Lion said "Watch over them and deploy defenses We have come too far to risk failure now "

"I assure you the gems—"

"You will guard them," Lady Dragon said "And you will not fail us in this "

She found her throat had gone dry "As you command, I obey "

"Yes " Lady Dragon severed the connection, leaving Mercia trembling all over

* * *

Terra stood, arms crossed, as they finally started digging in the ruin of the flophouse A week had passed since the fight with the bikers and the bomb squad had finally given the go ahead No one had seen any sign of Mercia after she left the airport Lin had gone to search for her and found a note with the ticket he bought her. The note read, "Hope you can get a refund." Terra's fist clenched. When she finally got her hands on Mercia...

She shook off her anger and focused. First the artifacts, then Mercia. The gauntlet at least had to be in there someWhere. Terra had no idea Why she couldn't sense it. Maybe some residual energy from her fire spell Was interfering With the detection magic

A huge excavator With a claW on the arm grabbed some of the rubble and spread it out on the ground nearby. Terra examined it through the glasses and found nothing. She shook her head and the operator gathered up the debris and dropped it in a Waiting container. For over tWo hours they repeated the procedure until they reached the concrete foundation. Someone had smashed a hole in it

Terra examined the hole and found a mixture of earth and dark magic in the dirt. She poked it and found the soil loose. Lin came over and crouched beside her. "Find something?"

"There Was a tunnel here, but it collapsed. The magic holding it together Was negated. I'll bet you our missing artifact is buried in that tunnel along With the biker from the hospital."

"That Would still leave us one short based on the video Lacy, I mean Mercia, provided."

"True, and We still have no idea Where those five cases ended up. What do you say We dig out this tunnel and see What We have left to find afterWard?"

Lin nodded and motioned the excavator over.

Three tedious hours later they had tWo bodies and the fire gauntlet. The magical Weapon Was every bit as poWerful as Terra had first thought. In the hands of someone that really kneW hoW to use it, a lot of damage could be done Not that the thug had been any slouch in the damage department, but in the hands of a fire wizard what he'd done amounted to nothing. She'd feel much better when it was locked up in the Department's secure storage room

Though they'd stopped digging when they found the bodies, the tunnel clearly continued on to a garage a little ways away. Lin drew his pistol and the two of them eased over to the building. Terra spoke a short incantation and the door slid up out of the way. Lin lunged in, weapon leading. Five bikes, including the one from the hospital, sat in the middle of the dirt floor.

While Lin searched the saddlebags Terra checked for magic. There was just a hint of dark energy around the bags, but that was it. "They must have transported the cases somewhere else."

"There's nothing here but more guns and a dirty bandana. Shit! Another dead end. We're running out of leads."

Terra chewed her thumbnail. "Where's the other bike?"

"What?"

"There are six dead bikers. Did any of those guys strike you as the type that would ride double? Where's the other bike?"

"'Scuse me."

Lin spun and raised his pistol

A skinny guy with black, lanky hair and covered in tattoos raised his hands. "I surrender."

Lin lowered his gun. "This is a crime scene. You're going to have to leave."

"Okay, but I had some information for you about the gang that lived over yonder"

"If you have some information for us, sir, we'd be most grateful if you passed it along," Lin said.

"I thought you might be. One of them badasses paid me two hundred bucks to give you guys an address on the off chance there was a fight at the house. I thought he was nuts, but it's three weeks later and I assume he's dead and you're here."

Lin and Terra shared a look. "What address?" Lin took out his notepad.

The informant rattled off a warehouse number on the docks. "He said you'd find what you were looking for."

"Why did you follow through?" Lin asked. "He's dead. You could have kept the money and not said a word with no one the wiser."

"Hey, man, when Tito gives his word and takes your money, he does the job."

The sun was low in the crimson sky when Tito wandered off the way he'd come. Lin and Terra headed back to the cars. Terra stretched and yawned as they walked.

"It's getting late," Lin said. "What do you say we head out to the docks in the morning?"

"Good call. If there was trouble I wouldn't be much use, tired as I am."

"I'll pick you up at your office at eight. Okay?"

Terra nodded, climbed into her car, and headed home. She'd be glad when this case was closed and she could return to her regular work. Being a policewoman exhausted her and she didn't even have to do the paperwork. She'd miss seeing Detective Lin Chang. A faint smile curved her lips. She should do something about that, assuming she found the courage.

* * *

The cry of gulls and the stink of a mixture of salt and rotten fish assaulted Lin the moment he stepped out of his car He put his hand over his nose, but it didn't help At all From her grimace Terra wasn't any more pleased with the odor than Lin She muttered something and swirled her finger around The stink vanished, replaced by a sweet, cinnamon odor

"I don't know what you did, but thanks "

"My pleasure, believe me "

They'd parked in an empty lot beside warehouse thirty-two, a rusted-out metal building with three condemned signs nailed to the walls He sighed Why couldn't these thugs ever do their dirty work somewhere nice Then again, if they ran into trouble he was just as glad the nearest people were the longshoremen working a quarter mile up the dock unloading a cargo ship

Further out to sea another pair of the huge container ships waited their turn to dock and unload One of them sounded a horn that echoed across the waterfront and sent the birds scattering

Lin and Terra headed toward the warehouse The main doors were covered in rust and bird shit It didn't look like anyone had opened them in a while

"I think Tito sent us on a wild goose chase " Lin shook his head

Terra raised her hand, closed her eyes, and cast another spell "No, there's something in there It looks like the missing motorcycle There are two more doors on the back side of the warehouse We can get in that way "

It Was a short Walk to the rear of the building. The back doors Were every bit as rusty as the front but scratch marks and a feW scuffed areas indicated they'd been moved recently. Scattered shafts of light pierced the darkness inside. Lin grabbed the door and yanked it open enough for them to squeeze through.

A light sWitch hung on the Wall a little Ways to the left of the door. Lin Weighed the chances of getting electrocuted then flipped it. Not so much as a spark.

"I'll handle the lights." Terra held out her hands and spoke a spell. Six gloWing pebbles appeared on her palm. She bleW a puff of air over them and they fleW up to the roof and greW bright enough to reveal everythIng In the vast space

Not that there Was much beyond the mix of empty beer cans, rotten scraps of food, and a torn mattress stained With god only kneW What littering the floor. A little Ways further on a black chopper rested on its kickstand. The bike had skull-embroidered saddlebags. Whatever they Were supposed to find Would be in those.

"Don't touch anything." Lin Worked his Way over to the bike, careful to folloW his oWn advice.

Lin reached the bike and flipped open the first bag. Another gun, terrific. HoW many Weapons did these guys have? The next bag yielded an envelope labeled "pig."

"I guess it's for me."

While Lin studied the letter Terra crouched and carefully reached inside the bag. "I found one." She spoke so softly Lin barely heard her

A black coffer identical to the ones from the videos rested in Terra's hand. It shined in the magical light. At first glance there appeared to be no seam. "Can We open it?"

"It's empty."

"How can you tell?" Lin moved in for a better look. He reached out to touch it

"Stop!"

Too late

His finger brushed the smooth wood and darkness descended on the warehouse.

The scream of a bird filled the air. Terra grabbed him by the collar and began to chant

A bubble of white energy surrounded them and pushed back the darkness. Movement flickered here and there.

Lin pulled his automatic, but couldn't find anything to shoot

"Put that away. Those are shadow beasts. Your bullets won't do anything "

Lin holstered his weapon. "What should I do?"

"There's nothing you can do. This is my fight."

Lin hunkered down behind Terra. His gaze darted back and forth, trying to figure out what sort of creature they were dealing with.

The answer came a moment later when a huge black raven slammed into the barrier and disintegrated. Terra flinched and her barrier wavered for a moment.

She chanted another spell, this one in the hissing language of fire. A dome of flame appeared over the white one already in place

Lin hated feeling so useless. There was more stuff in the bag and it was within her barrier. Even if he couldn't fight he could still investigate

He reached into the open bag. Inside was another envelope, a big manila one stuffed to the top and unlabeled.

"We have to make a break for it," Terra said. "Be ready to run."

Lin snatched the envelope and tucked it inside his jacket. "Where to?"

"Outside. If we can make it to the sunlight it will weaken the shadow beasts enough for me to destroy them."

"I like the sound of that. Say when."

She snapped her fingers and the flame dome exploded outward. Lin caught a glimpse of dozens of ravens swirling around. It looked like they were made of living darkness.

"Now!"

They ran for the open door

Terra stumbled on a pizza box.

The light barrier wavered as she struggled to catch her balance

Lin grabbed her by the elbow and around the waist and they ran on. The flames holding off the ravens flickered and began to die

Only a few strides to go.

He put his head down and pushed Terra along as fast as he dared

A raven slipped through the flames and slammed into the barrier. It burst and cracks appeared in their protection.

Two more strides.

Another raven flew at them. Lin pushed Terra out the door and into the sunshine a step ahead of it He staggered and spun around. A cloud of shadowy birds swirled around the warehouse. There had to be hundreds of them

Beside him Terra began another spell A ball of flame appeared above her head and continued to grow as she chanted

"Can you really destroy all those monsters?"

She ignored him and kept casting, her voice getting louder as the fireball grew With a final shout she hurled the sphere at the collection of shadow beasts It detonated in the center of the group

Lin looked away from the blinding explosion When he turned back the ravens and most of the warehouse roof were gone

Terra fell to her knees and wheezed, her bloodshot eyes leaking tears Her skin had turned ashen and her lips pale blue Lin had seen drowning victims that looked healthier

"You okay?"

She offered a weak nod "Used too much power with that last spell This is the backlash Give me some time "

"Can you make it back to the car? This is no place for a rest "

"Hurts everywhere You go ahead I'll be along as soon as I can "

"I'm not leaving you alone in your condition I can read standing up "

"Thanks " She fell over on her side and curled up in a ball

Lin didn't have a lot of experience working with wizards, but he'd never heard of one collapsing after using magic Not that it was probably something they advertised

* * *

Lady Raven sat at her desk, a tome bound in black leather open in front of her Two crimson, blood candles burned on either side of the book, shedding a flickering gloW over the tWisted Infernal script. Her Workshop apartment Was the only place her enemies hadn't discovered yet.

It Was rented in the name of another persona that had no connection to Lacy Winn or Mercia Bottomley, so she had no reason to think she'd be discovered. Still, her hunters had proven disconcertingly adept and determined. She Would have to be careful for the next year. One more mistake could jeopardize the project, not to mention her life.

She rubbed her eyes and refocused on the text. The black magic book had been her reWard When she achieved the rank of Sub-Hierarch tWo years ago. Lady Wolf had delivered it herself, a great honor indeed. If—When her current mission succeeded, Lady Dragon Would grant Mercia the privilege of joining the true Hierarchs. That Would be an even rarer honor, as feW ever met the secretIve leader of the SocIety face to face.

Lady Raven's head popped up When a distant Ward triggered. Had one of the shadoW gems been discovered? No, that Was impossible. They Were too Well hidden.

A full-length, black glass mirror hung on the Wall and Mercia Walked over to it. It Was vastly better suited to scrying than the simple bathroom mirror she'd been forced to use at the motel. She focused on the tingle in the back of her mind and spoke the Words of activation. "ShoW me What lies beyond my sight, Spirit Vision!"

The glass greW cloudy then resolved into an image of the docks.

Her shadoW ravens sWirled around a decrepit Warehouse. Lady Raven froWned. She hadn't hidden one of the shadoW gems there, in fact she'd never even seen the building before.

What in the world was going on?

"Closer." The image zoomed in. Detective Chang and Terra staggered out of the warehouse and onto the docks. What was she holding?

The image zoomed further. How had Terra gotten ahold of one of the coffers? Wait, that wasn't one of the ones she hid, that was the sixth that had held the gem she'd used at the carnival to try and kill Conryu. That should have been consumed along with the gem when the spell ran its course.

Goddamn useless bikers.

They must have kept it after removing the gem instead of leaving them together like she told them. But why? Iron Skull would never have disobeyed her. Lady Raven had had the great dumb thug wrapped around her finger. Not the other one though. What was his name, Bone? He'd always looked at her with suspicion. He had to be the one that betrayed her.

Back on the docks Terra cast a spell that destroyed her ravens along with a good-sized chunk of the warehouse. Perhaps she'd underestimated the quiet wizard.

Even if Terra was stronger than Lady Raven had thought, the wards she'd placed around the hidden gems were far stronger than the one she just bested and judging from Terra's condition that effort had about killed her.

If Terra continued to interfere she would finish the job her ravens started

* * *

Lin draped his suit coat over Terra as she lay moaning softly on the ground. The warehouse still smoldered and every once in a while a steel rafter would come crashing down. He'd called in the incident then turned his attention to the envelope marked "pig." Clearly whichever biker had left it here expected a member of the police to find Tito and eventually track the letter down. That spoke to a level of planning Lin wouldn't have expected from one of the brutal gang members

He tore open the envelope and pulled out a single folded sheet of paper. A note written in flowing script said:

Dear Pig. If you're reading this the bitch wizard has betrayed us. I knew she would, but Iron Skull refused to listen. She looked at us the way I look at roaches. I've set up this somewhat elaborate treasure hunt both to conceal my work from Lady Raven and to see if you have the brains and determination to carry out my revenge. Since you're reading this I assume you do.

Lady Raven had one major job for the gang and that was to place five boxes like the one you found throughout the city. We each took one to a specific location. After we placed it she must have cast a spell on us, because I can't remember any details. I've spoken to the others, all except Iron Skull, and pieced together as much as I could. It's all gathered in the second envelope.

I don't know what the witch has planned, but I'm certain it's nothing good. Not that I care, you understand, but no one betrays the Black Skulls and gets away with it. One of our boys already died doing the wizard's errands. Stop the bitch and avenge my brothers, Pig.

It was signed "Bone" and beside the name was the image of a stylized skull. It seemed Mercia wasn't as well loved as she might have hoped. Whichever of the dead bikers was Bone Skull, Lin owed him a thank you.

Terra groaned behind him and he turned to find her struggling to her feet Sirens in the distance heralded the approach of the police and fire departments The area would be crawling with people soon Once Lin gave his report he'd leave the cleanup to others Terra staggered over and returned his jacket Her lips were pink again and she'd stopped crying

"You good?" he asked

"No, but I'm better " Terra leaned on him as they walked back to his car to wait for backup to arrive He quite liked the feeling "Anything interesting?"

Lin handed her the paper

When Terra had finished reading she said, "Lady Raven, huh? That explains the shape of the defensive ward Though I can't prove it, I'm certain it's Mercia Have you looked through the other papers yet?"

"No, I was going to wait until I got back to headquarters " The first fire truck pulled in "I'll have to explain what happened then we can head out That reminds me How come the trap went off when I touched the box, but it ignored you?"

"I didn't touch it "

Lin stared "You picked it up "

"I conjured an energy barrier between my bare skin and the coffer It's standard procedure when handling an unknown magical device You can understand why "

"You might have warned me "

Terra shrugged "I tried, but I wasn't quite fast enough It never occurred to me that you might try and touch it We're trained in how to handle magical items I guess I assumed you were too See what comes from making assumptions? From now on we're going to have to be much more careful "

Lin couldn't argue with that.

* * *

"I don't believe the threat is over, Captain." Lin sat in front of his boss's cluttered desk and tried to remain calm. "Just because the bikers are dead doesn't mean we're finished. The letter clearly states that the wizard, Lady Raven, still intends us harm"

Lin had dropped Terra off at the Department of Magic and continued on back to his station. The moment word got out that he was back his commander called him into his office and gave him hell for destroying the warehouse. It was mostly pro forma since the thing had been condemned anyway. What wasn't, however, was his captain's very real desire to have this case be closed. A pile of dead thugs made for an excellent ending, one he could show the mayor and get a pat on the back in return.

The captain liked a good pat on the back, but Lin couldn't sign off on the case when he knew those boxes were still out there.

"Lin, I understand, really. But this is now a matter for the Department of Magic. Our part is finished. Turn over all your information to them and move on. We have a backlog of murders as long as my arm that need investigating"

"Sir, I really don't think we should leave this investigation unfinished. The risks are too great."

"You've been working this case, what, a couple weeks nonstop? Take the rest of the day off, tomorrow too, then come back in ready to start on something new."

"Sir—"

"This isn't a debate, Detective. Go home."

Lin got up, nodded, and reached for the door

"Lin "

He turned back "Sir?"

"You did good work on this case The Black Skulls were wanted in three other sectors for crimes ranging from murder, to arson, to kidnapping Getting them off the streets is a huge deal Don't think I don't appreciate it "

"No, sir It's just I don't think the job is finished and I hate leaving something half done "

"The wizards will take care of their own Regular folks like us will only be in their way "

After the mess he'd made of things at the warehouse Lin didn't have a good argument for that one "Understood, sir If they need us I'm sure they'll let us know "

Lin took his leave, pausing at his desk to collect the letter and packet Terra was smart and hard working He had no doubt she'd get to the bottom of whatever was going on Probably better than he'd have done it himself

His battered pickup was parked at the far end of the crowded lot The long walk helped clear his head He had a day and a half, maybe he could still help, at least for a little longer The starter whined when he turned the key, but it finally caught

The station was only ten blocks from the government complex so five minutes later Lin was parking again He collected his evidence and marched through the main doors Only one of the secretaries had a customer so Lin chose the farthest-in slot and walked up to the man behind the desk

"Can I help you, sir?"

Lin flashed his badge "Detective Lin Chang to see Terra Pane "

"One moment, Officer." The man picked up his phone and punched three digits He murmured something, nodded, and hung up. "She's with the chief. You can head on up. His office is on the top floor."

"I don't want to interrupt."

"It's okay, Chief Kane wants to speak to you as well. The elevators are in the back to your right."

Lin took the elevator up. A short hall led to a closed door. Behind a desk to the left of the door sat an attractive woman in her mid-thirties. She brushed her brown hair out of her eyes and smiled "You can go right on in, Detective"

"Thank you." Lin nodded to the woman in passing then tugged the door open

Inside was a spacious office with a glass wall overlooking the city. The floating island was still visible far out over the ocean. Two walls were lined with bookcases. Directly ahead was a huge cherry desk behind which sat a broad-shouldered bald man that had to be Chief Kane. In one of the two chairs in front of the desk he recognized the back of Terra's head.

The chief stood up and walked over to the staring Lin. "Come in, Detective No need to be shy"

Chief Kane shook his hand and guided him over to the empty chair. "Sit down, make yourself comfortable. We're all friends here"

"Thank you, sir." Lin settled gently into the soft leather chair. It probably cost more than his truck.

"Orin, please. I know you and Terra are already aquatinted. She tells me you've been a tremendous help in trying to locate Mercia"

"That's why I'm here" Lin placed the documents on Orin's desk "My captain says as far as we're concerned the case is closed Dealing with Mercia is a matter for wizards"

Orin smile vanished. "Is that right? What do you think?"

"I don't think we should close out the case, but it's not my call The plain truth is I'm a very small fish in a big ocean If the captain says I'm done, I'm done"

"We'll see about that" Orin picked up his phone and dialed a number A moment later he said, "Tom? It's Orin, I need a favor Of course we're on for golf this Sunday I wouldn't miss it"

"Who's he talking to?" Lin whispered to Terra He was relieved that her color had returned to normal

"Probably the mayor They're old friends I suspect very shortly you're going to be back on the case And thank god for that"

"Why? I'm sure you could have handled it"

"I'm a researcher, Lin I don't know the first thing about criminal investigations I've consulted once or twice, but I never ran one on my own If the chief dropped this in my lap I wouldn't know where to start"

"Thanks, Tom" Orin hung up the phone "There, that's all sorted out You'll be getting a call shortly, Detective Until then how about you show us what you brought?"

Lin handed him the letter "I haven't had a chance to even open the packet yet Have you examined the box at all?"

Terra shook her head "Nothing more than a cursory look It'll take me weeks if not months to fully reconstruct the spell from the residual energy At first glance it strongly resembles the energy from the carnival ritual. I assume at one time it held Whatever catalyst Lady Raven used to activate the spell. If I use that as a starting point it might speed things up a great deal, unless I'm Wrong, in Which case it'll set me back."

Orin shook his head and dropped the letter on his desk. "Not terribly encouraging, Terra. And this letter is too vague to be of much use "

Lin's cell rang, interrupting Orin. He looked at the Department chief Who nodded. "Detective Chang."

"No," his captain said "Lieutenant Chang "

"I don't understand, sir."

"You're being promoted and reassigned as liaison to the Department of Magic. You'll also serve as their chief investigator. Congratulations " The captain hung up

"Good neWs?" Orin asked.

"I guess. I've been reassigned to your department as chief investigator." Lin's head spun. He'd Worked out of the same station since he joined the force. He kneW everyone there and they kneW him; some of them Were like family.

"We can alWays use good people at the Department." Orin handed him the letter. "Terra, I believe there's an office up the hall from yours That should be a good place for the detective. Get him settled in, Won't you?"

"Yes, Chief "

Terra groaned and stumbled to her feet. Lin folloWed her example. Orin shook his hand again and Terra led him out of the office.

Just like that his Whole career had changed. Lin had Wanted to finish What he started, but What Would happen after?

How much use did the Department of Magic actually have for a detective?

He followed Terra out and back to the elevators. They rode down to the fifth floor where she guided him to a closed door. Terra opened it and a musty smell mixed with bleach washed over him. Lin stared at the so-called office. It looked more like a storage closet. Someone had shoved a cheap particleboard table and plastic chair into it and rechristened it an office. There wasn't even a computer or shelves. Hell, he didn't even have paper and pencil. On the other hand it had four walls and a door, which put it head and shoulders above the cubical he'd worked out of at the station.

"I know it doesn't look like much," Terra said. "But I can get you a Department laptop and there's a supply closet down the hall, just help yourself to whatever you need. I'm right next door if you have any questions."

Terra ducked into her office down the hall and closed the door, leaving Lin to his own devices. First things first. He tossed the letter and packet onto the table and went to fetch a notepad and pencil. Getting to the desk was a squeeze, good thing he stayed in shape. If he was ten pounds heavier he doubted he'd fit.

The contents of the packet spilled out onto his desk. Page after page of handwritten notes in the same hand as the letter. Lin scanned the first five, trying to get a feel for what he had. It looked like Bone had simply written down everything the other members of the gang remembered about their missions. There was no rhyme or reason and most of it lacked context.

One said he remembered mostly birds and trees. That could describe any one of a hundred parks in the city. Another described rushing Water, but Was it the seWer or the Gallen River entering the ocean? HoW Was he supposed to make sense of this?

Epilogue

Lady Raven stretched and got up off her couch. For the past ten days, since Terra and Detective Chang had discovered her box in the Warehouse, Lady Raven had been going from one hiding place to the next, setting additional Wards and preparing guardians. It seemed next to impossible that the hiding places Would be discovered, but if they Were Whoever found them Would regret it.

There Was one more matter to attend to. While her apartment Was comfortable and secure for the moment, she couldn't discount the possibility of her enemies learning about it. If they did it simply Wasn't possible to protect it the Way she'd like, at least not Without draWing attention that she didn't Want. She needed a secure fortress she could retreat to When the time came to activate the ritual. SomeWhere her enemies Wouldn't dream of trying to breach.

She had a location in mind and nearly a year to prepare HoWever, before she'd fully Warded it the building remained vulnerable. Guardians would be necessary for the first month or two, then as a second line of defense. The multiple failures of her shadow beasts had demonstrated their limits in the starkest terms, especially when it came to sunlight.

If she eliminated that weakness, their power was beyond question. What they needed was a shell to protect them from the weakening rays of the sun, and Lady Raven knew exactly where to find such hosts.

She shrugged on her black robe and chanted, "Reveal the way through infinite darkness. Open the path. Hell Portal!" A black disk appeared in the air before her. Lady Raven stepped through it and into the borderland between the mortal realm and Hell. Time had no meaning in this in-between place and distance was simply a matter of will.

With her destination firmly in mind Lady Raven called the name of a demon she knew. A black-winged monster appeared out of the darkness and carried her to her destination. She spoke the spell again and emerged in a darkened corner outside the government building

It was late and the sky moonless. No figures stirred in the night. Her former place of employment would be empty, but Lady Raven had a different destination. An invisibility spell hid her from anyone she might encounter as she made her way to the city offices. In the basement of that building was the morgue where unclaimed bodies awaited cremation.

There should be a handful of night watchmen patrolling the grounds, not that mere men would have any chance of stopping her, even if they could see her Five minutes later brought her to her destination. While the guards weren't an issue, the wards protecting the building were another matter. The moment she stepped through the doors her invisibility would be stripped away. Worse, she couldn't open a portal inside either.

She smiled. If there weren't challenges what was the point of doing something? She marched up the steps and stopped in front of the glass doors. Inside, a single guard sat with his chair leaning back against the wall, his feet up on a hard wooden bench.

Lady Raven knew the security routine as well as anyone who had ever worked there. Assuming they hadn't changed anything, another three guards should be patrolling the other floors while this fool guarded the lobby. In reality they were probably all holed up somewhere napping. That's what happened when you hired minimum wage workers to protect your property. As long as she made it past the first man without raising a ruckus the rest would be easy.

A hard rap on the glass got the guard to spring to his feet. He stared at the entrance, but of course couldn't see her. He narrowed his eyes then rubbed them, as if that would make any difference.

Come on, you great buffoon, come investigate.

The guard shrugged and started to settle back in. Lazy, useless excuse for a guard. She thumped the glass again, harder this time. He whirled around and stared again. Finally he pulled his flashlight and started for the doors.

Lady Raven chanted, "Your life is mine." Her hand crackled with necromantic energy as she stepped aside to avoid bumping into him.

The guard unlocked the doors and stepped outside. He waved his flashlight this way and that, trying in vain to figure out what had made the noise. He was a young man, barely older than Conryu.

When he turned back toward the doors she reached out and grasped the back of his neck. The dark energy flowed out of her hand and into his head. Flesh withered and rotted, leaving nothing but a skull sitting atop his broad shoulders.

The guard collapsed and she left him where he lay, stepping over his body and through the now-unlocked doors. Her skin tingled as her invisibility spell was negated. Lady Raven marched through the empty lobby, her hard heels clicking on the tile floor. She went straight to the elevator and rode it one floor down to the basement.

The elevator chimed and the doors slid open revealing a fully equipped surgical suite. The overwhelming scent of disinfectant mingled with a hint of blood. It appeared someone had just cleaned. She hoped her former servants were in good enough condition to house the shadow spirits.

Beyond the operating room was the morgue. Dozens of niches sealed by stainless steel doors covered the back and side walls. She brushed aside the hanging plastic barrier and went straight to the rear wall. A quick scan of the labels revealed the Skulls' resting place.

Lady Raven gestured and spoke a word. Five doors opened and the slabs slid out revealing the pale, tattoo-covered bodies of her former servants Each of their torsos sported a stitched up Y incision. Two of them had nasty burns covering their arms and back and a different pair was riddled with bullet holes.

They made an especially unattractive group of potential servants, not that they'd been much more appealing while still alive. Still, the corpses Were sufficiently intact to serve as hosts for her Faceless Ones and nothing else mattered.

Lady Raven began the summoning spell "Spirits of death and darkness, faceless foes of the living, appear and serve me."

The already chill air dropped another tWenty degrees as she tapped the corrupt energy of the netherWorld. Her spell reached a crescendo and five humanoid figures made of living darkness appeared above the corpses. The Faceless Ones oozed into the bodies, filling every pore and orifice until it appeared the bodies had been dipped in an oil slick.

SloWly the nether spirits Worked their Way into their neW hosts. All around her the other niches began to rattle. One door popped open and a foot emerged. Like a sort of bizarre birth, a mindless zombie Worked its Way free of the narroW slot. In short order a second and third emerged, animated by the residual energy of her summoning spell

These Weak, stupid creatures Were of no use to her beyond the annoyance they'd cause her enemies When they came to Work in the morning. A simple command spoken in Infernal sent the neWly made zombies out of the morgue and out of her Way. They'd shamble around in the basement, maybe a feW Would find the stairs and Work their Way up, folloWing the scent of the guards patrolling the upper floors.

Before the Faceless Ones finished integrating With their hosts tWenty of the lesser zombies had shuffled out of the morgue. The clumsy things sent tools crashing to the floor in the surgical area as they made their Way out.

When the last of the crashes sounded and the moans had faded to nothing, Lady Raven checked on the progress of her guardians. The black essence of the Faceless Ones had sunk fully into the bikers' bodies. The wounds had sealed, leaving the flesh smooth and free of punctures. This wasn't done for aesthetic reasons, but to keep any light from reaching the spirits and potentially weakening them.

The process of entering the flesh would also serve to transform it, making the skin durable enough to withstand bullets and the bones hard enough to survive the impact of a truck. When they reached her soon-to-be fortress Lady Raven would make further improvements to her guardians.

"Rise," she commanded

The five once-faceless spirits forced their hosts up off the slabs. Their movements were stiff at first, though already smoother than the zombies. That was to be expected. The spirits had been bodiless for a long time. It would take weeks for them to grow fully used to having a physical form again.

She grimaced at their thoroughly ugly, nude bodies That would need to be remedied as soon as possible. "Follow me."

* * *

Orin sat at his desk and held his head in his hands as Adam finished his report. The night before someone had broken into the district office morgue and raised all the bodies inside. The undead had proceed to kill the four night watchmen and a handful of employees before the security forces were called in to destroy them. They'd gotten lucky in that the creatures were among the weakest sort of undead and required only a bullet to the head to put them down permanently.

"So that's it," Adam said. "Five bodies are still unaccounted for. We've searched the whole building so our working assumption is that whoever made the zombies took the bikers' bodies away with them."

Orin looked up. "You mean she, not they. Can there be any real doubt that Mercia is behind this?"

"I agree that she's the most likely suspect, but since we have no proof it's still speculation. Do you have any further orders?"

He sighed and shook his head. "Not for the moment. Though we'll certainly want to increase our patrols and make sure no one walks their route alone."

"I already made the adjustment to the schedules. If there's nothing else I'm going to make a final inspection of the building so everyone can return to work."

Orin motioned him out. When did his life get so complicated? It didn't seem that long ago that his biggest worry was Maria getting another ear infection. Now he had the first male wizard to deal with, a deranged former employee breaking in and stealing bodies, and his little girl going off to college in five weeks.

He rested his head on the cool wood of his desk and sighed. That felt good

The door opened and he looked up to find Terra striding toward him, looking grimmer than usual. She stopped in front of his desk and leaned forward. "I found where she opened a portal. There were footprints in the grass leading up to it."

"When did you become a tracker?"

"The tracks killed the grass right down to bare dirt. A blind person could have followed them."

"Fascinating, but I hardly think dead grass is our biggest concern right now."

"Then you're mistaken" Terra's scowl deepened "Whatever Mercia transformed the bikers into has a powerful enough dark aura their presence alone was enough to kill the grass That means they're also strong enough to drain the life from a person and there are five of them god only knows where out there"

Orin rubbed his face and swallowed another sigh "What do you propose we do about it?"

Terra's expression softened "I've been thinking about that ever since I found the tracks The truth is I have no idea"

"That's not what I was hoping to hear from my chief researcher Speaking of which, have you made any progress on the box?"

"I understand the function of the box itself It was designed to hold something, hiding its aura until a specific condition caused it to open In this case the spell has been modified so only a specific individual would be able to open it I assume the missing boxes retain the initial enchantment"

"Does any of that help us?"

"Not really"

Orin thumped his head on the table Of course it didn't This summer had been a comedy of errors, why should it change now? They just needed a tiny bit of luck and it would break everything open, he knew it in his bones Luck, unfortunately, had been in short supply

The Impossible Wizard

Author Notes

I hope you've enjoyed the first book of my new series. It was a lot of fun to write. I'd been wanting to do an urban fantasy for a while now, but when I settled on The Aegis of Merlin story line I decided I was going to write a story my way, multiple points of view and third person POV. It was a risk since a lot of urban fantasy is written from the first person POV. I think the results are quite good and maybe something a little different from what's out there. That was my goal anyway. If you'd like to learn more about me and my books I encourage you to head over to my website. WWW.JAMESEWISHER.COM You can read my blog posts, check out the other books I've written, and sign up for my newsletter.

Until next time, thanks for reading.

James E. Wisher

About The Author

James E. Wisher is a writer of science fiction and Fantasy novels. He's been writing since high school and reading everything he could get his hands on for as long as he can remember. This is his tenth novel.

Made in the USA
Monee, IL
12 April 2021